RONAN'S CAPTIVE

HIGHLANDER FATE BOOK TWO

STELLA KNIGHT

PRONUNCIATION GUIDE

Ronan - ROE-nan
Eadan - AE-dan
Beathan - BEH-un
Suibhne - SOOEE-nyuh
Luag - LOO-ak
Moireach - MOE-ruch
Tarag - TA-ruhg
Uallas - WAL-us
Neasan - NES-an

CHAPTER 1

Present Day
Syracuse, New York

Kara entered the dusty old attic and took it in. This was her grandmother Alice's domain when she was still alive, with the stacks of books and old boxes arranged just the way she preferred. Kara had avoided the attic while she was growing up, finding the endless stacks of books overwhelming.

Taking it in now, Kara could almost see Alice huddled in the corner chair, poring intently over one of her books about medieval history, straightening to give Kara a kind smile.

But Alice, as her grandmother insisted she call her by her first name, died two weeks ago, and as her only granddaughter and sole heir, it was up to Kara to sort through all of her belongings. She'd cleaned out Alice's Craftsman-style home every day for the past two weeks and purposefully avoided the attic until now. It held too many memories; Alice's presence infused every book, every box, every corner of the attic she'd spent so much time in.

Kara expelled a breath and stepped into the attic, squatting down on her haunches to begin the arduous task of clearing it out. The distant relatives who'd come to Alice's funeral offered their help in clearing out Alice's home, but Kara had refused. In a way, these were her final moments with her grandmother; so much of Alice lingered in this house even after her death.

Kara smiled as she picked up an old photo album, cringing as she flipped open to an old photo of herself. In the photo, she was fourteen, gangly and awkward, her braces visible as she smiled at the camera.

Kara placed the photo album into the "KEEP" box. Sentimental to a fault, she suspected Alice kept every single embarrassing photo of Kara's embarrassing adolescent years.

Alice had stepped in to raise Kara after her mother's death from cancer; Kara was eight at the time, an only child who'd never known her father. Alice was a young grandmother, only in her late forties when Kara came to live with her. Alice often told her she believed fate brought Kara to live with her; she'd loved Kara fiercely.

"I miss you, Alice," Kara whispered, blinking back a wave of tears as she picked up a framed photo that lay beneath the photo album. It was one of Alice from her younger years; her blonde hair long and flowing, free of the gray that would eventually wind through it, the green eyes Kara had inherited bright and vivid, her lips turned up in that familiar half-smile she often wore.

Alice had been ill for some time with a heart condition, but her death still hit Kara hard, adding more misery to a decidedly crappy year. The magazine where she'd worked had laid her off from her job as an investigative reporter, a dying gig in an increasingly dying industry. Kara loved her job and was a full-fledged workaholic, throwing herself into every aspect of her job to the fault of everything else—including relationships. But Alice never criticized how much her granddaughter worked, even when such work caused her visits to decrease. Alice simply told her one Thanksgiving that there would come a day when work wouldn't seem so important. Kara had tried not to roll her eyes, assuming Alice was referring to the magical moment when she'd meet her future husband—something Kara didn't think would ever happen. Kara was twenty-nine and hadn't yet met anyone who piqued her interest as much as her job; her last boyfriend told her he felt as if she was cheating on him with her job, and it would always come first. Deep down, Kara suspected he was right.

Kara fanned herself with an old book, expelling a sigh. She'd only been out of work for a month but it seemed like ages. She couldn't wait to find another job to throw herself into, something to distract herself from her grief.

Taking out her phone, Kara scrolled to an upbeat playlist to listen to while she continued to sort through Alice's things. She made good progress for the next two hours, sorting stacks of books, journals and photo albums into the "KEEP" and "DO NOT KEEP" boxes until she reached the back corner of the attic.

There, she spotted a wooden chest sealed shut with a combination lock. Tucked away beneath several other boxes, it looked as if someone had tried to hide it away. Kara studied it, baffled. She may not have spent much time in the attic, but she didn't recognize it at all.

Kara pulled the chest out of the corner, noticing a small note affixed to the top.

For my granddaughter Kara Forrester's eyes only.

Her confusion deepened. Alice had mentioned nothing about this chest during her last few visits, and if anything valuable was inside, she hadn't included it in her will.

Kara reached down to tear the note off the chest, flipping it around. Alice had scrawled another message.

Care Bear, if you're reading this use the special password.

Kara couldn't help but smile at her grandmother's use of her childhood nickname, one she continued to use well into Kara's teen years. As a teen, Kara hated the nickname, but now a wave of painful nostalgia washed over her. She'd do anything to hear Alice call her "Care Bear" again.

She looked down at the combination lock. She knew exactly what password Alice referred to. It was the date she'd come to live with Alice, a date Alice said had changed her life for the better.

June 12th, 1996. 6121996.

Kara turned the combination lock to the corresponding numbers of the date. As she spun the dial to the final number, it gave away and she opened the chest.

Surprise filled her as she gazed inside the chest; only an envelope and garment bag were nestled there. Her brow furrowing, Kara reached for the envelope.

She tore it open, removing a letter that was at least ten pages long. Kara leaned back against the wall to read.

Care Bear,

I've been investigating a historical family mystery for some time; something I uncovered while researching our genealogy. In the spring of 1390, records indicate a fire occurred in the middle of the night during a clan conflict in the Scottish Highlands. A separate branch of our family died in this fire. I've only been able to find scant records about it, but it looks like the fire was purposeful and killed many; the perpetrators were never found. Our distant ancestors were just innocent bystanders.

Kara lowered the letter, rubbing her eyes.

While this was tragic, she didn't know how this letter warranted Alice locking it away with a note telling her it was for her eyes only.

She kept reading.

You know I can't resist a good mystery—just like you, Care Bear. I began investigating this particular region in the Scottish Highlands around the time of this fire, and there were rumors of people vanishing —and appearing out of nowhere.

Kara stilled, but made herself keep reading.

I think I know the reason for those disappearances. Stay with me, sweetheart, because this is going to sound crazy. I believe time travel is real. And . . . I can't tell you how I know this, but I believe you have the ability to travel through time.

Kara's hands shook as she reread this part of the letter several times.

"Oh, Alice," Kara whispered, lowering the letter and pressing her hand to her mouth. Alice had been logical to a fault; she didn't believe in anything without hard evidence. She hated science fiction and anything under the fantasy umbrella.

Unease swirled through Kara's gut. Alice's mind had been clear to the very end; the doctors told her she was in no way cognitively impaired. It looked like the doctors were wrong.

Kara swallowed, forcing herself to keep reading.

I know what you're thinking, Care Bear. That your grandmother has lost her marbles. Now, all I have as proof is hearsay and rumors. But I always trust my gut instinct and I want you to humor me. There are coordinates at the bottom of this letter; they're in Scotland. In the garment bag there's a dress that will suit where you're going.

And if I'm not crazy and you are indeed pulled back through time—I'd like you to put those investigative skills of yours to use. I want you to solve this mystery and save the lives of our distant ancestors—and the countless others who died that spring.

CHAPTER 2

1390
Macleay Manor

"She was here," Beathan insisted, turning to face Ronan. "The lass. I swear it."

Ronan met the desperate eyes of his steward, his mouth tight. He'd left his cousin Eadan's wedding early to return to his manor after his servant Gavin had fetched him. Beathan had sent for Ronan after seeing a strange lass wandering the grounds. A lass who supposedly vanished before his eyes.

But they'd spent the entire evening checking every section of the manor's expansive grounds, from the stables to the back gardens, even patches of the surrounding forest, but there was no sign of a wandering lass.

"I know it sounds mad," Beathan continued, at

Ronan's wary look, "but the lass vanished. I saw it. I
—I think 'twas one of the *stiuireadh*."

Ronan stiffened. It seemed like he and Eadan
were the only ones who didn't believe in the
stiuireadh, druid witches who supposedly made
people disappear.

Beathan kept his imploring gaze trained on
him. Disappointment coursed through Ronan as he
met Beathan's dark eyes. In his fiftieth year, with a
kindly round face and paternal manner, Beathan
was one of the most rational men he knew; it was
one of the reasons he'd hired him to oversee his
manor.

"'Tis likely a lass who got lost and made her
way back to the castle—or the village," Ronan said
with a dismissive wave of his hand. "The castle's
not far; it may be a wedding guest who lost her
way."

Beathan didn't look convinced, but Ronan
turned to make his way back to the manor. Earlier,
he had every intention of returning to the castle
after searching for this mysterious lass, but the
fruitless search lasted longer than he'd thought and
the wedding festivities had likely ceased by now.
Eadan would have long since taken his new bride,
Fiona, to their marital bed.

Eadan and Fiona were heading to one of the
Macleay properties deep in the Highlands for some
time alone after the wedding; they had a turbulent
few weeks dealing with the scheming of a rival clan
leader, Dughall of Clan Acheson. Eadan had told

Ronan he wanted time alone with his new bride before stepping into his role as chieftain of Clan Macleay. While Eadan was away, he'd entrusted Ronan with leadership duties of the castle and the clan. The next day Ronan would officially take over Eadan's leadership duties. Anxiety filled his chest at the thought.

While Ronan held high rank in the clan and had a manor of his own, Eadan was the one who'd always shouldered much of the leadership responsibilities of the clan. Ronan was not a direct heir and didn't have the same pressures as Eadan; he'd spent most of his life enjoying his leisure with lasses, drink, and sport. But deep down Ronan envied his cousin for his admirable leadership skills; Ronan didn't believe he possessed the same talents.

As Ronan entered his empty chamber, stripping out of his kilt and tunic, a wave of envy swept over him as he thought of Eadan's newfound happiness with Fiona. This envy had first pierced him during their wedding and continued to linger, which irritated him. He'd never desired a bride of his own, relieved that the pressure was all on Eadan to produce an heir for the clan.

He realized that he'd not bedded a lass in weeks with his attentions focused on the conflict with Clan Acheson. He'd just have to find a bonnie lass to sate his lust soon. Once he quelled his restless loins, this odd longing of his would cease.

~

AT FIRST LIGHT the next morning, Ronan made his way on horseback to Macleay Castle. Tension gripped him as he arrived, entering the great hall. A dozen yeoman, tenants, and landholders had already gathered; all eyes fell on him as he made his way to the head table.

On a daily basis, Eadan heard their grievances and issued resolutions. If he couldn't come up with a resolution on his own, he'd hold a meeting with the other clan nobles. Ronan was glad to not have this duty, but in Eadan's absence this was now Ronan's role.

For the rest of the morning, he listened to the concerns of each man. Thankfully, they were minor disputes over land and crop yields, and Ronan issued what he hoped were fair resolutions.

Relief filled him as the crowd began to thin, though his eyes widened in surprise at the raven-haired woman who stepped forward, the last visitor of the day. Elspeth Graeme. The widow of a high-ranking noble of Clan Macleay, she'd also been a sympathizer and close ally of Clan Acheson. Eadan and his men hadn't found her guilty of any wrong-doing in the days after the battle with Dughall, but she was still not without suspicion. Eadan had ordered her to remain under watch by his men, and her movements beyond clan lands were restricted.

"Mistress Graeme," he said politely, though his body had gone rigid with tension. "Do ye have a grievance I can assist ye with?"

Elspeth paused before speaking, giving him a

seductive look with her dark eyes. Elspeth was a frequent guest at suppers at the castle; during one such drunken supper Ronan had kissed her. He'd not gone further than that; while she was quite bonnie, she didn't stir desire in his belly and he hadn't tried to bed her. But by the surreptitious glances she cast him whenever she was around, he knew she desired more.

"I've come tae request ownership of lands in the south owed to my late husband, Artagan Graeme. My request has been under consideration for some time, since before the battle with Dughall and his men."

"I'll review Eadan's land deeds, but I may need tae wait for my cousin's return."

Elspeth's mouth tightened and she clasped her hands before her.

"Aye," Elspeth murmured. "I understand, m'laird. But I hope it doesnae take much longer, I am owed those lands. I'd be grateful if ye could send me notice when the lands will be signed over. Or . . . ye could pay me a visit at Graeme House."

Her words were polite but heavy with meaning. She smiled, her gaze lingering on his. Ronan averted his eyes, trying to keep his expression stoic. It was foolish of him to ever kiss the lass and give her false ideas.

"I will send word when I can," he said. "I thank ye for coming tae the castle."

Elspeth's face fell with disappointment but she

gave him a respectful nod and left the hall, trailed by a female servant.

"Yer cousin doesnae want tae grant Mistress Graham those lands; she's still not trusted."

Ronan looked up at the new steward of Castle Macleay, Moireach, who'd sat silently at his side all morning. Now Moireach glowered at him with a look of disapproval.

"I made no promises," Ronan stiffly replied. "As I told her, I'll wait for the laird's return."

Moireach gave him a curt nod, getting to his feet.

"There're deeds and rents tae be looked over in the laird's study. Come," Moireach said, not waiting for Ronan as he headed out of the hall.

Ronan glared after him. Moireach had replaced Eadan's former steward Naoghas, a kind man Ronan had known since he was a bairn. Dughall had Naoghas killed weeks ago; Ronan, Eadan and many in the clan missed him greatly. Moireach came recommended from the household of another clan noble, and while he proved to be more than competent, he was already acting like an overbearing father, one who didn't respect Ronan's temporary leadership.

Ronan spent the rest of the day reviewing the stacks of parchments on Eadan's table in his study; he didn't even have time to break for a midday meal. He didn't know how his cousin handled such a tedious task day in and day out.

Night had fallen when Ronan finally returned

to his manor, tucked away on its own patch of land a small distance away from the castle, its dark gray stone veneer looming in the darkness as he approached.

His uncle had granted him the manor in his twentieth year after the previous owner passed away. And while he spent most of his time there, it never felt as much of a home as Macleay Castle did. He'd grown up in the castle, his uncle Bran having taken him in after the death of his own father. Bran was more like a father to him than an uncle, Eadan a brother.

A sudden stab of loneliness pierced him. Eadan and Fiona would soon start their family and Bran had retired to his own home off castle grounds. Soon the castle would no longer feel like home. He supposed this was why men chose to wed—to create a sense of home. It wasn't something Ronan had even pondered nor was it something he'd ever wanted. He didn't want to bear the responsibility of a bride, a family. His series of mistresses brought him great contentment, and he made certain to tell each one before he bedded them he had no desire to wed.

Ronan dismounted from his horse as he arrived in the courtyard of his manor, handing the reins to a stable boy who rushed forward. There hadn't been time today, but he intended to hold a supper at the castle to seek out his next mistress. He'd make it clear what he was looking for—a lass to warm his bed. Just because Eadan settled down with a wife didn't mean he had to do the same.

Appeased by the thought, he entered the manor and climbed the stairs, heading down the long hallway to his chamber.

He froze at the sight that greeted him. At the base of his chamber door lay a piece of charred wood. He recognized the darkened bark, wood from an elder tree.

It was an ill omen—and someone had placed it there for him to find.

It was a threat.

CHAPTER 3

Present Day
New York City

During the train ride back to New York, Kara's thoughts kept returning to her grandmother's letter. The things she'd written were crazy, but Alice had been completely lucid and levelheaded the last time she'd seen her.

Kara closed her eyes, rubbing her temple and leaning her head back against her seat. There was a part of her that wanted to believe Alice hadn't written the letter, that someone had placed it in her attic as some cruel practical joke.

But she knew her grandmother's handwriting like the back of her hand.

I believe time travel is real.

Kara opened her eyes, her gaze straying to the chest she'd stored beneath her feet, the chest that contained the letter, along with a fourteenth century-era gown Alice wanted her to wear when she magically traveled through time.

Kara recalled her childhood fear of ghosts, and Alice's repeated assurances that ghosts—and anything supernatural—didn't exist. *I guess time travel doesn't count.*

As her train pulled in to the bustling Penn Station, Kara decided that she would just store Alice's chest in her living room closet. She ignored the guilt that flared in her chest, but she could hardly do what Alice asked. Time travel wasn't real, and her request was ridiculous. Insane. Why couldn't Alice have had a simple last request, like be happy and live your life?

But Alice wasn't a simple woman. Even as frustration and disbelief coursed through her, Kara smiled at the memory of her grandmother's unorthodox personality.

Alice had been a history professor at Syracuse University, specializing in medieval studies. Kara had met some of her students who told her about Alice's nontraditional teaching methods. Instead of lectures, papers and exams, Alice would gather her students in class, her home, parks, or wherever struck her fancy, and hold detailed back-and-forth conversations about medieval history. She'd also been a nontraditional guardian, never ruling over Kara with an iron fist, encouraging her to do whatever she wanted in life that made her happy.

"It's your path, Care Bear," Alice had told her

several years ago. "You already know where you're going and what you want."

When Kara entered her studio apartment in Brooklyn, she was still smiling at the memory. She set her suitcase down and marched the chest over to her living room closet, stowing it away in and closing the door, as if the act alone would push the chest from her thoughts.

Well, this is my path, Alice, she said silently. *To not entertain crazy ideas.*

She spent the rest of the afternoon unpacking, cleaning the mess she'd been too grief-stricken to deal with before she left and resuming her fruitless job search online. The entire time she took great effort to not linger on her grief or her confusion over Alice's letter; but the letter kept intruding into her thoughts like a pesky itch she couldn't scratch.

I want you to solve this mystery and save the lives of our distant ancestors—and the countless others who died needlessly.

Kara shut her laptop closed, getting to her feet. She wouldn't let herself entertain Alice's words. She wouldn't.

But the thoughts remained even after she crawled into bed, snatches of Alice's letter echoing in her mind. Unable to sleep, Kara slid out of bed around midnight and went to the closet to pull out the chest, feeling like a drug addict seeking her fix.

She took out the letter and read it once more, then again, before falling asleep on the couch, the letter clutched to her chest.

When she awoke the next morning, she knew she couldn't go about her usual routine of heading to the gym, returning to her apartment to job search, grocery shopping, then more job searching. The contents of Alice's letter had dominated her mind. And Alice knew her well—too well. Kara could never resist a good mystery to solve. It was one reason she'd become an investigative reporter.

Kara got to her feet, reaching for her phone. No more ruminating on her own. She needed outside advice.

She sent a quick text to her friend Jon, her former co-worker from the magazine. She and Jon had gone out on one bad date in which they'd discovered they had zero chemistry, but they did have great compatibility as friends. Jon was one of the most logical people she knew. While she didn't intend to tell him all the explicit details of Alice's letter, she'd tell him enough for him to give her advice.

Jon responded almost immediately to her text, agreeing to meet her for lunch at a nearby bistro. He met her outside the bistro, his dirty-blond hair mussed, as if he'd been raking his hands through it, his brown eyes filled with concern. Stepping forward, he gave her a long embrace and murmured his condolences.

Once they were seated, she kept the conversation light, telling him about details of her trip upstate as she tried to figure out how to broach the subject of Alice's letter. But midway through their meal, Jon set down his fork, his face infused with concern.

"Something's wrong," he said. "What is it?"

Kara studied him, taking a breath. How to word this?

So my grandmother's final wish is for me to go back in time over six hundred years and despite my best efforts, I'm actually considering it.

"I have a—question for you," she hedged. "Do you believe in . . . aliens?"

Her face flamed as the waiter refilled their glasses with water just as she asked the question. The waiter's face remained impassive, but his lips twitched.

Jon's eyes widened with both amusement and surprise. She waited for the waiter to leave before continuing. "Fairies? Monsters? Things most people don't consider real?"

Now Jon's amusement faded, and he studied her with growing concern.

"Kar, what's—"

"I'm just curious," she interrupted. "Humor me."

"Well," Jon said, after a long pause, "the short answer is—no. The long answer is . . . anything's possible. There's a lot we haven't discovered yet. And—what's that Sherlock quote? When you've excluded the impossible, whatever remains—"

"However improbable, must be the truth," Kara finished. She leaned back in her chair. But that was the problem. Time travel was impossible. Wasn't it?

"There—there's something Alice wants me to try," she said, as Jon pinned her with a probing look. "Something she requested in a final letter. Something I think is impossible . . . but I'm feeling guilty for not doing it."

"I suppose you're not going to tell me what this impossible thing is?"

"No," she admitted. "Sorry."

"OK," Jon said, raking a hand through his hair, his eyes filling with a patient understanding; he wasn't going to push. Kara smiled at him, relief flowing through her. She was glad she'd contacted him. "What's the downside to trying this thing she wants you to do?"

Kara considered. She would lose a few days from her job search. And she'd have to take money from her increasingly meager savings for a plane ticket to Scotland.

But if she did go, it would at least assuage her guilt over ignoring Alice's final plea. And she'd get a vacation out of this whole bizarre thing. She couldn't remember the last time she'd taken a vacation.

"Thanks," she said. "You've just helped me make my decision."

"You're . . . not going to go seek out aliens, are you?" Jon asked, looking so genuinely concerned that she had to laugh. "Fairies? Monsters?"

"No," she said, still chuckling. *Try time travel.* "When I get back, I'll tell you what Alice asked me to do. Trust me, you'll laugh."

"Well," Jon said, returning her smile with a shrug. "I look forward to it." He held up his glass of water. "To the impossible."

"To the impossible," she echoed, clinking her glass with his. *To time travel.*

~

Present Day
Larkin, Scotland

THE NEXT DAY, Kara was on a flight from JFK to Aberdeen International Airport. She'd felt ridiculous as she packed the fourteenth-century gown in her suitcase, but she reminded herself she was doing this for Alice. And, selfishly, to quell her guilt and curiosity.

She arrived in Aberdeen in the late evening and rented a car from the airport to drive to the small town of Larkin, the closest town to the coordinates Alice had provided.

Though it was dark, she could make out the stunning landscape of the Highlands around her: the dark rolling hills, the patches of forest in the distance, the glittering night sky. For some reason that she couldn't pinpoint, a chill settled over her as she drove deeper into the Highlands, along with the uncanny sense she'd been here before. Alice had taken several research trips to Scotland, but she'd never invited her along, and Kara had never come to Scotland on her own.

Now Kara wondered why. Had Alice somehow known all along that she'd one day ask Kara to do something like this?

Kara sighed, pushing the thought from her mind. There was no use filling her mind with even more questions.

After arriving at the quaint bed-and-breakfast in Larkin, the only one in the tiny town, she stayed up late reading and rereading Alice's letter, as if it would reveal new information, information that would answer the plethora of questions swirling around in her mind.

The next morning she dutifully put on the gown Alice had provided. She'd seen Alice wear similar clothing for reenactments she did with the local historical society, so she knew to start with the underdress, then the tunic, and finished with the lavender gown. She'd thought the gown would be uncomfortable—but it was far more comfortable than she'd expected, the fabric soft against her skin. Alice had told her corsets didn't become a thing until the sixteenth century, and for that Kara was grateful.

Not that it matters, she told herself. She would take this gown off as soon as she returned to the bed-and-breakfast and begin her vacation in earnest.

Kara eyed herself in the mirror. She'd tucked her honey-blond hair back in a messy bun, and anxiety filled her green eyes.

"This is how much I love you, Alice," she murmured.

Before leaving her room, she tucked a large pashmina around her body to avoid curious looks from the other guests. Fortunately, it was gray and drizzly outside so the pashmina didn't seem too odd.

She used her GPS to take her to the coordinates Alice had provided. She veered right on the forked road that took her deeper into the Highlands until she arrived at her destination.

Taking off her pashmina and storing it in the backseat, Kara took in the sight with surprise. She'd arrived at the ruins of what appeared to be a medieval village. There were no tourists or signs. It was completely desolate.

As she got out of the car, another chill settled over her, the type of chill that slithered through her whenever she walked down an empty street late at night. A sense of looming danger.

She hesitated by the side of her car. She could just climb back in and drive away; she'd come to the coordinates as Alice had asked. Alice hadn't provided any detailed instructions beyond that.

As she lingered, hesitation rendering her still, the wind suddenly picked up around her and she could have sworn she heard a faint whisper in the breeze.

"Kara."

Kara's heart picked up its pace. It was a woman's voice with a strange accent she didn't recognize. Her throat went dry as she looked around, but she was the only soul in sight.

Unease seized her, but something else filled her chest as well. A pull. She found herself stumbling forward, as if she were a magnet drawn to its source, toward the ruins of a castle on the edge of the village.

"Kara."

That whisper again. Shaking, Kara arrived at the ruins of the castle, looking around as she stumbled into the courtyard, but there was no one. Was she just hearing things?

The wind increased around her, tugging at her body, her gown and hair whipping around by its force. She had to reach out to grasp the crumbling castle wall to maintain her balance.

Fear crept down her spine as she noticed that neither the nearby trees nor the grass around the castle moved with the force of the wind; it was as if the wind was localized only to the castle. She heard Alice's voice—her words from the letter. *I believe time travel is real.*

With panic swirling through her veins, Kara turned to leave the ruins, but it was nearly impossible to move with the force of the wind pulling on her body.

And like invisible hands, the wind jerked her backward. She screamed as the world around her dissolved in a dizzying blur . . .

CHAPTER 4

1390
Macleay Manor

After finding the ill omen outside his chamber door, Ronan spent most of the night questioning his servants, trying to determine if any of them had seen a stranger entering the manor. Beathan looked furious when Ronan told him of the ill omen, vowing to help him find the perpetrator. But none of the servants they'd questioned had seen anything amiss.

Beathan seemed suspicious of their ignorance, but Ronan trusted his servants. He treated them well, and they were loyal to him and the clan. Many had worked at his manor the entire time he'd been laird.

"Donnae forget that Dughall's men turned some of Eadan's servants against him, and they were loyal as well," Beathan cautioned, after Ronan questioned the final servant and they stood alone in his study.

"If one of them is the traitor, I'll find out," he said, though he wasn't sure how. "I want a guard on the front and back entrance—'til this is sorted."

Beathan left him alone, and Ronan took a seat at his table examining the piece of burnt bark. The elder tree wasn't common in the Highlands; it needed more fertile soil. Many in the Highlands believed spirits lived in these trees and to burn them was an ill omen. Ronan did not believe in such superstition, but he believed in the sender's intent. Someone had taken great effort to seek one of these rare trees, burn its bark, and leave it for him to find as a warning.

That night he drifted off to sleep with troubled thoughts plaguing his mind. A banging on his door early the next morning roused him.

"M'laird!"

Ronan sat up, alarmed. It was Beathan's voice; he sounded panicked. Ronan shrugged into his clothes before hurrying to the door.

"What is it?" he asked, swinging it open to find a wide-eyed Beathan.

"There's another lass wandering the grounds— a different one this time," Beathan said.

Ronan closed his eyes, his shoulders sinking with annoyance.

"We already searched the grounds for— "

"This one didnae disappear," Beathan interrupted. He moved past Ronan to the window, peering out. "She's still there."

Ronan trailed Beathan to the window, stiffening as he followed his gaze. There was indeed a lass emerging from the forests on the far edge of the grounds—he couldn't make out any of her features beyond her golden hair.

Confusion filled him, and then fury, as he recalled the burnt elder wood he'd received the night before. Had she been the one to do it?

"I'll handle the lass," Ronan said, his mouth tightening as he stepped back from the window.

Moments later, he stalked out of the front door, making his way toward the lass. She stood frozen on the edge of the grounds and didn't try to flee.

As he drew closer to her, his mouth went dry. She was by far the bonniest lass he'd ever seen— hair the color of burnished gold, a heart-shaped face with a generous mouth and eyes a deep green that reminded him of a verdant meadow. She was tall for a lass, her slender curves pronounced beneath the lavender gown she wore. He felt himself harden against his kilt as hot, molten desire filled every part of him.

Christ, Ronan, he scolded himself. *She's an intruder on yer lands. Now's not the time tae think with yer cock.*

"Who are ye?" he demanded, once he reached her. "Why are ye intruding on my lands?"

The lass just looked at him, a stricken look in

her eyes. Her gaze flitted past him to the manor and back to him. She swallowed but said nothing.

"I'm going tae ask ye again, lass," he said, stepping forward, close enough to inhale her scent—cinnamon and rosemary. He ignored the swell of desire that surged over him, keeping his voice firm. "Who are ye and why are ye intruding on my lands?"

"My—my name is Kara," she stammered. "I'm —I'm from the—er—the village. I'm lost."

Ronan went still as he studied her. She had the same strange accent as Eadan's wife Fiona. His suspicion spiked as his gaze raked over her gown. The village was some distance away on foot, and her dress was that of a noble woman's. Noble women didn't live in villages—they lived in manor homes or castles. And they certainly didn't go around unescorted. The lass was lying to him.

"I'll ask ye again, lass," he growled. "Who are ye?"

"I told you," she said, her voice firmer now, her chin jutting upward with defiance. "My name is Kara, and I'm from the village. I'm lost. Could—could you point me in the right direction?"

Ronan's eyes narrowed. More lies. He stepped forward and took her arm in a gentle but firm grip. She let out a yelp as he dragged her toward the manor, struggling to get out of his grasp.

"Let me go!" she shouted. "This is—HELP! Let me go!"

He shot her a look of disbelief as they continued toward the manor.

"Ye're trespassing on my property, lass," he growled. "No one will help ye except me. And I willnae be doing that 'til ye tell me who ye are."

He continued to drag her into the manor, past the small group of servants who'd gathered in the entry way, keeping a firm grip on her arm as he led her up the stairs and into a guest chamber at the far end of the hall.

Only then did he release her, closing the door behind him and leaning against it with his arms crossed.

Kara stumbled back from him, looking around at the chamber like a frightened deer. Ronan's anger subsided; she seemed genuinely frightened.

"I'll not hurt ye, lass," he said gently. "I'm Ronan of Clan Macleay, laird of this manor. Now I ask ye only for the truth. Who are ye?"

"I told you—"

"The truth."

Kara blinked, and her eyes glistened with tears. His heart softened with sympathy, but he reminded himself of the ill omen he'd received the night before. How could it be mere coincidence that she'd shown up the morning after he received it? He needed to be on guard.

"All right," she said, taking a deep breath. "I'm —I'm here to look for my family."

He studied her. He suspected she was still

withholding something, but this statement seemed truthful.

"I—I arrived at a village. Somehow, I made a wrong turn, and I ended up here. I'm—I'm sorry I trespassed on your grounds, but I didn't know where I was. I just—I just want to be on my way."

"Yer family? What are their names?"

"Suibhne and Orla," she said. "They're farmers. They have two young daughters."

Ronan searched his mind, but the names were not at all familiar, and he knew dozens of the villagers by name. Her face fell, which confirmed for him she was telling the truth—at least about searching for her family.

"I'll need tae confirm yer telling me the truth," he said. "And then . . . perhaps ye can be on yer way."

"Perhaps?" she echoed, stiffening with alarm.

"Aye."

"And until then?" she demanded. "You can't mean to keep me prisoner here?"

"As ye were trespassing on my property, 'tis my right," he growled. "'Till I can confirm what ye say is truth . . . ye're my captive."

CHAPTER 5

*Y*e're my captive.

The Scot's words reverberated in her mind as he shut the door behind him, and she heard a lock turn in the door. Kara stumbled back and sank into the bed, pressing her hand to her mouth, her heart hammering.

This can't be real. This can't be real.

But it was. That ridiculously gorgeous Scot—sporting authentic medieval clothing she recognized thanks to Alice. The servants, also in authentic period clothing. Even this room, with no hint of electrical outlets, just a candle holder on the side table.

Kara swallowed, leaning forward to press her forehead against her knees. Everything had happened so fast. The sound of her name whispered with the wind. The wind tugging on her body. The world dissolving around her.

When the world righted itself again, she'd

found herself on the outskirts of this manor. She'd barely had time to orient herself when that tall, muscular, golden-eyed Highlander stalked toward her, demanding to know who she was in that heavy Scottish brogue she'd struggled to understand. And now . . . she was his prisoner. The captive of a living, breathing medieval Scot.

Kara sat up, taking a breath. There had to be some logical explanation. She looked around, searching for any sign of the date. Hurrying over to a side table, she pulled open a drawer, finding a prayer book. She flipped it open searching for a date. And though it was in Latin, she understood the year, written in stark lettering on the parchment.

1390.

"Holy shit," Kara whispered, as the room spun around her. "Oh my God."

Alice was right. Somehow . . . she'd been pulled back through time.

She took a seat on the bed when her legs began to wobble, trying to connect her haphazard thoughts. Evidence that she was in the past—the authentic clothing of the Scots. Ronan's accent, different from modern Scottish English. As Ronan dragged her into the manor, she'd looked around, seeing no hint of paved roads or cars. But then again, she'd been distracted by Ronan's beauty. She'd never met a man she would call "beautiful" before, but Ronan fit the bill. Strong, chiseled features, wavy chestnut hair, golden eyes. His body was all lean muscle, and he moved with the grace of a panther.

Kara pushed away her lustful thoughts, shaking her head. The man was holding her prisoner, for crying out loud.

She stood, moving over to the window. In the courtyard below, a man mounted a horse and rode away. In the near distance, a carriage made its way down a winding dirt road. She continued to scan the surroundings, praying she'd see a car, a plane, anything that would indicate she was still in the twenty-first century. But all evidence indicated that she was indeed in the past. Over six hundred years in the past.

An avalanche of questions filled her mind. How did this all work? Why did she arrive at this manor? Did the whisper of her name on the wind have something to do with it? Had it been that wind that sucked her back through time? How did Alice know Kara could time travel? How did she know where to send her?

And another, more prominent question—why hadn't Alice told her sooner? Why did she wait until after her death to deliver such a bombshell?

Because you wouldn't have believed her, a phantom voice whispered. She had to admit this was true; Kara would have seriously considered placing Alice in a hospital if she'd told her such a tale when she was alive. Besides, Kara was so consumed with her job during her grandmother's last years, she wouldn't have entertained such a story by coming to Scotland anyway.

Pushing aside her guilt, Kara forced her thoughts back to the present. She had two choices here—figure out how to get back to her own time, which would mean figuring out how to get back to that abandoned village. She could only assume that the means through which she'd traveled was there; maybe it was some type of portal.

Or. She could do what Alice sent her here to do. And for Alice to want her to *travel through time*, it must be a damn important cause.

Suibhne and Orla. Those were the names of her ancestors Alice had provided in her letter. Surnames weren't common in this time, especially among peasants and farmers. She only knew that they were in their late twenties at the time of their deaths, and they had two young daughters.

She thought of Suibhne and Orla, along with the others who'd died in this time, and a surge of turbulent emotions filled her. How could she not save innocent lives if she had the opportunity to do so? And there was the investigator in her that wanted to solve the mystery of what happened.

A sense of resolve settled over her. She needed to accept that she'd somehow traveled through time. If she could honor her grandmother's dying wish and save lives . . . she would do it.

But first, she needed to convince Ronan that she was trustworthy.

Ronan returned to her chamber a couple of hours later with a young chambermaid. Kara had used the time to come up with what she hoped was a good enough story to convince him he could trust her.

She took him in, swallowing. He trained his beautiful eyes on her face with wary caution.

"Ye can leave the tray on the table, Aislin," he told the chambermaid, still studying Kara.

Aislin obliged, casting Kara one last curious look before leaving them alone.

Her throat went dry as he approached, and she took a breath to calm herself. This would be a lot easier if he weren't so distractingly gorgeous.

"No one in the village recalled a lass who looks like ye," he said, his eyes narrowed.

"I—I'm sorry I wasn't truthful with you before. I was startled and frightened. My—my grandmother recently died," she said, her voice wavering. There was no need for her to put on an act about that, genuine grief shaped her tone, and tears stung her eyes. A fierce longing for Alice's presence filled her; her grandmother would know exactly what to do in this situation.

Ronan's eyes softened, though his body remained rigid.

"My apologies for your loss," he murmured.

"There was a branch of our family she was close to, but she lost touch with them over the years," she continued. "Before she died, she asked me to find them. When we last heard from them, they were just settling into the village here. It was her dying request, one I intend to honor. I did get lost; I was trying to find my way to the village. I only had enough coin for the coach I hired to drop me off here; the driver refused to take me any farther and told me the village was just up the road."

She held his gaze, hoping that he gleaned the partial truth in her words. But his expression remained guarded.

"Where are yer things? Ye traveled with just the clothes on yer back?"

Think, Kara.

"Our coach was robbed by bandits on the road outside of Edinburgh," she returned, trying to look appropriately shaken. Bandits were a common danger travelers had to deal with in this time.

Ronan's mouth tightened, but his face remained unreadable; she couldn't tell if he believed her or not.

"And what were ye planning to do in the village?"

"Inquire about my family at the church."

"If they're not at the village?"

"Then I'll return home," she said, though she had no idea how.

"Home. Where is that, lass?"

"England," she lied. English sounded much

different in this time, but it was the best she could come up with under the circumstances.

He studied her for a disconcertingly long moment before speaking again.

"All right," he said, and relief coursed through her. "But instead of staying in the village . . . ye can make yer inquiries from here. There's plenty of room for ye. Ye can stay as my guest."

"But—"

"We've just had a . . . disagreement with another clan, and there may still be traitors among the clan. I believe some of what ye say, lass, but yer hiding something. I'll not take any chances."

Kara glared at him. Damn him for being so perceptive. She'd gotten as close to the truth as she dared. There was no way she could tell him she was from a different time. Alice had told her that witch hunting and the belief in witches was very much a thing in the fourteenth century. If she was going to save her family, she needed to stay alive.

She bit her lip, looking around at the spacious chamber. It wasn't like he was keeping her in a dungeon. Staying in a sprawling manor a hundred times the size of her Brooklyn apartment wouldn't be so terrible. It had to be better than making her way into the village and asking around on her own, especially with the difference in accents and language.

Still, unease filled her at the thought of staying here. Ronan was gorgeous, but he was a stranger.

And she didn't believe for one second that she was just a "guest." He didn't trust her.

A small part of her briefly considered escaping, finding her way back to that village through which she'd arrived and traveling back to her own time.

But memories of Alice flowed through her mind. Her gentle smile the last time she'd seen her. Her heartfelt letter. *I want you to solve this mystery and save the lives of our distant ancestors—and the countless others who died needlessly.*

She would do this for Alice. Even if she had to deal with an irritatingly handsome and distrustful Highlander to do so.

"Fine," she said. "But as soon as I find my family I'll be on my way."

"Perhaps," Ronan said silkily, suspicion lingering in his eyes as he moved closer, until he stood only inches away. Kara tried to keep her expression neutral, but awareness coursed through her at his close proximity.

"I'm not here to do anyone harm," she said, "I just want to honor my grandmother's wishes."

"It would be simpler for ye tae just tell me the truth, lass."

"I—am," she whispered.

His amber eyes seared hot on her face, and her awareness spiraled into desire, seizing her by the throat. She was close enough to fully appreciate his masculine beauty—those bright fiery eyes, sensually full lips, the hint of stubble that lined his jaw. His eyes dropped to her lips, and the silence between them shifted, becoming charged with heat. He was so close now, close enough to . . .

"There's a meal for ye," Ronan said abruptly, stepping back and turning away from her. He gestured toward the tray the chambermaid had placed on the table. The charged moment dissipated; Kara had to take a second to collect herself, drawing in a ragged breath.

"I'll have a chambermaid bring ye more clothes."

And then he was gone, leaving her with a gnawing, unquenched desire.

CHAPTER 6

*R*onan gritted his teeth with frustration as he walked away from Kara's chamber. He couldn't believe he'd nearly kissed a lass he didn't trust. But that generous mouth and startling green eyes of hers had drawn him in, and it took everything in him to turn away from her. He needed to bed a lass to rid himself of this searing lust—and soon.

A sudden image of Kara in his bed, her blond hair splayed around her like a halo, naked, moaning as he stroked her heated center, filled his mind.

He shut out the image from his thoughts. He'd have to stay away from the tempting lass—at least until he determined her true identity.

His thoughts strayed to Fiona, Eadan's bride. It seemed too much of a coincidence that two lasses with similar accents would show up on Macleay lands within weeks of each other. While there was no doubt in his mind that Fiona was trustworthy, as she'd helped them defeat Dughall and his men, he wasn't so sure about Kara. What was she hiding?

As soon as he entered his study, he sent for Beathan.

"Who is the lass?" Beathan asked, his eyes sparkling with interest. "She's bonnier than the one I saw before. Does she need an escort somewhere?"

He didn't like the lustful gleam in his steward's eyes, and he got to his feet, towering over him.

"No. The lass will be staying here. She's . . . a friend," he said carefully. "I'll not have her spoken of with disrespect," he continued, his voice coming out harsher than he intended.

"I'm sorry, m'laird," Beathan said, his round face coloring with contrition. "I meant no disrespect."

A sliver of guilt filled Ronan; Beathan had meant no harm. It made no sense that he felt such possessiveness over a lass he'd just met.

"I ken ye didnae," Ronan said, with a conciliatory nod. "But I have a task for ye. I need ye tae send a messenger tae the village and inquire about her family. She's searching for them."

Beathan obliged, leaving him alone. Ronan looked down at his table where he'd left the ill omen. Did Kara have something to do with this? Had she been the one to send it—and was she working with some new enemy?

He sat down, leaning back in his chair. The lass was hiding something, but something told him she wasn't here for a nefarious purpose. She was telling the truth about looking for her family and her grandmother. Instinct told him that whoever sent the ill omen was someone else. Someone dangerous.

He searched his mind, trying to recall any other clan or family that Clan Macleay had come into conflict with. As far as he knew, Clan Macleay had good relations with other nearby clans.

But Ronan hadn't paid much attention to such matters. Such conflicts had been all Eadan's concern, and before that, his uncle's. A sudden desire for his cousin's presence shot through him. Eadan was a born leader. He'd know how to handle this—and how to handle Kara's arrival.

When Fiona had arrived out of nowhere, Eadan promptly had her pose as his bride—and fallen in love with her during the whole charade. Ronan had no intention of doing something similar with Kara. Unlike Eadan, he wasn't trying to get out of a deceitful betrothal. But he was determined to keep her at his manor until he found out who she was. Eadan and Fiona would return in a few weeks' time. Given the similarity of their accents, perhaps Kara was from the same village as Fiona, and Fiona could find out who she truly was.

Eadan and Fiona are also hiding something, a voice in his mind reminded him. He'd suspected there was more to Fiona's backstory, but when he'd pressed Eadan, he evaded the question. What was Eadan hiding for Fiona? And was it linked to whatever Kara concealed?

Ronan got to his feet, heading out of the study. There was no use for him pondering matters he had no answers to. He needed to focus on the identity of the sender of the ill omen—not on whatever Kara was hiding. He'd have to deal with that later.

He needed to question Clan Acheson members and members of Clan Macleay who'd sympathized with their cause, but received a pardon from Eadan. And he knew just where to start.

He had Beathan put a guard on Kara's door, ignoring the stab of guilt that pierced him for doing so. But the lass could have her freedom when she told him the truth. He took a horse and rode east to Elspeth's home. Given her closeness to Dughall's daughter and other members of Clan Acheson, if there was a renewed plot against Clan Macleay, he hoped Elspeth's attraction to him would make her tell him of it.

Elspeth looked up with surprise and delight when he trailed her servant into her drawing room, where she was working on a piece of embroidery. She dismissed the servant with a wave, and he noted with irritation that she jutted out her bosom as she got to her feet and approached him. He may have found her bonnie in the past, but compared to the mysterious foreign lass imprisoned in his manor, she might as well have been an old unattractive man.

He gave her a polite but guarded smile, not wanting to encourage her attentions. He needed to make it clear why he was here.

"Ronan," she said, stopping only inches away him. "I'm so glad ye've come."

Ronan nodded, taking a small step back from her. It was subtle, but sent the message he wanted to get across—he was here for official reasons only. Disappointment flared in her eyes but she maintained her smile.

"I need tae ask ye about Clan Acheson," he said. "In yer talks with Magaidh, or any of the clan members, did they mention any allies? Anyone Dughall was working with?"

The disappointment in her eyes shifted to something dark and unreadable. She turned away, making her way back to her chair.

"No. I've already told Eadan's men when they questioned me—I didnae ken what they were planning. But no one believes me; 'tis why I'm a prisoner in my own manor."

"Ye're not a prisoner," Ronan said, though her words weren't far from the truth. But she needed to earn the clan's trust after her entanglement with Dughall and his clan.

She wasn't looking at him now, her hands folded in her lap, her mouth set in a firm line.

"Elspeth, I'm just asking if ye ken of any allies Dughall may have had. Anyone outside Clan Acheson and Clan Macleay who may have wanted tae do us harm."

"They didnae include me in such talks," Elspeth said, her voice clipped. "I wouldnae ken if they had."

She still wasn't looking at him; instinct told him she was hiding something. Anger seared his chest; he was growing weary of lasses not telling him the truth.

"Elspeth, if ye ken anything, it would be best tae tell me. Ye're right, there are some in the clan who think ye should've been punished, who think ye ken more than ye let on. If ye're honest with me, that can only help ye."

"I am being truthful," she said, her eyes flashing as she shot to her feet. "I'd do anything tae prove my loyalty tae Clan Macleay."

She again approached him, her smile sly and seductive, reaching out to place a hand on his arm. Unlike the rush of heat that flowed through him when he touched Kara, Elspeth's touch left him cold.

"I'm disappointed that ye've only come tae discuss clan business," she said, her voice dropping to a purr. "I was hoping yer visit would be of a more . . . personal nature."

She smiled and stepped even closer, so that her breasts nearly touched his chest, leaving no question of what she was offering.

Though he felt nothing at her proximity, a devious thought entered his mind. *'Tis been some time since ye've bedded a lass. Bedding Elspeth will help keep ye away from Kara.* And perhaps Elspeth would tell him what she was hiding if he bedded her.

But he forced away the thought. He'd not fiddle with her emotions that way—and Elspeth did nothing to stir his loins. Once again, an image of Kara appeared in his mind's eye, her face flushed, her lips parted as her eyes met his, and a rush of desire coursed through him. How could the mere thought of Kara fill him with such fire when the presence of another lass, one who desired him, leave him so cold?

Elspeth smiled triumphantly at the desire in his eyes, misreading it as desire for her. She stood on her tiptoes to press her lips to his, but Ronan stepped back.

"If ye recall anything," he said, "ye ken where tae find me."

This time, the disappointment in her eyes turned to hurt. But he'd not bed the lass and make her believe he harbored feelings he did not have.

"Aye," she said shortly, turning away from him, her voice turning cold. "I will."

Ronan headed to the castle. He decided not to tell the other clan nobles about the ill omen he'd received; he wanted to capture the perpetrator on his own first and he didn't want to cause undue alarm. Nor would he tell them of Kara's appearance; they'd want to question her, and a surge of protectiveness filled him at the thought. If he thought Kara was suspicious, he could only guess what the nobles would think of her, especially in light of the recent conflict with Dughall.

At the castle, he tended to the matters of the day—payments to the castle workers, deed signings, inquiries and concerns from tenants on Macleay lands. The entire time, his thoughts kept drifting to the foreign lass back at his manor.

For the first time in a while, he looked forward to returning to Macleay Manor.

When he returned to the manor that evening, Beathan approached as soon as he stepped into the entryway.

"I sent the messenger tae the village as ye asked," Beathan said. "But no one he asked had heard of or noticed a married couple by the names of Suibhne and Orla."

Disappointed on Kara's behalf, he gave Beathan a nod of thanks. He headed to Kara's chamber, dismissing the guard who waited outside and entered.

Kara had changed into another gown the chambermaid had brought her, this one a shade of green that brought out the color of her eyes. She stood by the window, looking out at the darkened grounds that surrounded the manor, her expression turbulent.

She turned when he entered, her face tightening with defiance. He wanted to smile; he admired her spirit, and just the sight of her sent a spiral of heat careening through him.

"My messenger found no evidence of yer family in the village," he said.

Kara's shoulders sank, disappointment filling her eyes.

"I see," she murmured. "Thanks for checking."

Ronan studied her, hesitant. He didn't want to say the next words, but he wanted to be fair to the lass.

"Do ye need coin tae continue on yer journey?"

"You're going to let me go?" she asked, her eyes narrowed with suspicion. "I thought you didn't trust me."

"I donnae," he returned coolly. "But as long as ye're not on Macleay lands, ye're not my concern."

"And if I do remain on your lands? I need to stay in this area until I find them."

He smiled, a ripple of pleasure flowing through him. *Good*.

"Then I insist," he said, taking great effort to keep his voice firm, "that ye stay."

Her mouth tightened and she looked away.

"Then I suppose I have no choice," she muttered.

"Ye'll be my guest—or my captive. The choice is up to ye, lass," Ronan said gently. "Supper will be served shortly. A servant will come fetch ye."

"I suppose I have to eat with you as well?"

"Aye," he said, ignoring the stab of hurt that pierced him at her question, his tone turning cold.

If she wanted to treat him as her captor, so be it.

CHAPTER 7

*K*ara tried to concentrate on the meal in front of her, but it was difficult with Ronan's intense gaze on her face.

Earlier in the day, when she realized he'd put a guard on her door, fury had coursed through her. Once her anger subsided, she'd spent the day ruminating, from recalling every detail she could about Alice's letter, to considering how to flee the manor to get back to her own time, and finally resolving once again to stay. She couldn't have innocent deaths on her conscience. She'd just have to work harder to get Ronan to trust her.

She looked up at Ronan and forced a polite smile. Their meal comprised of smoked herring, roasted carrots sweetened with honey, and bread. To her relief, spoons existed in this time, though she noticed that Ronan used his fingers and a knife to eat, something she tried her best to mimic.

Kara had wondered what a medieval meal

would taste like; she knew from Alice that only the wealthy ate well in this time. This appeared to be true, the herring was as tasty as a dish in a pricey New York restaurant.

"Thank you for the meal," she said, deciding it was better to soften him up before bringing up the guard on her door. "Very delicious."

"My cook is one of the best in the Highlands," Ronan replied, but his expression remained guarded.

"I can tell," she said, taking a swallow of her ale, which was far more bitter than she'd anticipated, but she kept the smile pinned on her face. "So . . . am I to have a guard outside my chamber the entire time I'm here?"

"Ye can wander the manor and the grounds. But I'll continue tae have someone watching ye."

Kara's smile vanished. She glowered at him, gritting her teeth. She reminded herself that it would do no good to make an enemy of him. She needed Ronan on her side if she wanted to find her ancestors. He'd already helped her by having his messenger inquire about her family's whereabouts in the village. If she got on his good side, maybe he'd continue to help her.

So she made herself give him an understanding nod and forced another smile. Surprise flared in his eyes; he'd clearly expected a fight. He returned her smile; desire rippled through her at the sight. His smile made him even more beautiful.

"I understand," she said. "You want to protect

your lands, your clan. I'm a foreigner; it makes sense for you to be on your guard. But I'm not here for any other reason than to find my family."

"That I believe," Ronan said, setting down his cup and steepling his fingers beneath his chin.

"Well. It's good you believe me about that," Kara said, trying to keep the bitterness from her voice. "This is a lovely manor," she continued, opting to change the subject.

Make the subject comfortable by establishing a rapport. This was something she'd done during her time as an investigative reporter. Hopefully her technique would work on a fourteenth-century Highlander.

"This home has been in the Macleay clan for generations, along with the castle. I was raised by my uncle; he gave me this manor by inheritance," he replied, leaning back in his chair as he took a long sip of his ale.

She wanted to ask him what happened to his parents but didn't want to push too much. She decided to change tactics, offering more information about herself instead. The more truthful information she gave him, the more he would trust her. Or at least she hoped.

"I lost my parents when I was young," she said. "My grandmother raised me. She was more like my mother *and* my father."

"And that's why finding this family is so important to ye?"

"Yes," she replied, her voice wavering.

"Who do ye live with . . . in England?" he asked, his eyes narrowed. "Ye donnae have a male guardian who'll miss ye? A husband?"

Kara scrambled to think. A woman living alone in 1390, unless a widow, was a rarity.

"My grandmother only recently died, I intend to move in with my uncle once her affairs are settled," she said, hoping she sounded truthful. "He knows I've traveled to Scotland and he gave me his permission to come. He'll not expect me back for some time."

Ronan studied her for a long moment, his face blank. She couldn't tell if he believed her story or not.

"I wonder about ye, lass," he said finally. "I believe what ye say about yer grandmother and finding this family—there's nothing but truth in yer eyes. But there's much ye say that's false; I can also tell by yer eyes. Ye say yer English, yet yer accent . . ." He trailed off, his eyes boring into hers. "My cousin just wed a lass with an accent akin tae yers."

Kara stilled, her heart thundering in her chest. He didn't know the accent he referred to was an American accent. And his cousin had married someone with such an accent.

Could it be? Was there another time traveler here? Or was it a coincidence, and this woman he spoke of just happened to have an odd foreign accent he didn't recognize?

"It is a rare accent," she hedged, wondering how to get more information about this woman without being too obvious. "Where's your cousin's wife from? Perhaps we're from the same village."

"At first she told us she was from a small English village. Now. . . I'm not sure where she's from," he continued, watching her with razor-like focus. "My cousin refuses tae tell me. But she claims her accent is odd because she traveled a lot as a wee lassie."

Kara tried to maintain her calm, clenching her palms in her lap. A woman in this time with an American accent and a vague backstory? Sounded like a time traveler to her.

She tried not to let her excitement show, reaching out to lift her cup to her lips and taking another sip of ale.

"I also traveled a great deal when I was young, but I'm from the southern coast of England," she lied. One area of medieval history Alice had never been great at was the linguistics of the time, so Kara was on her own here. "Is—is your cousin's wife nearby? At the castle, perhaps? I'd love to meet her. See if we traveled to the same places as children."

"Fiona and my cousin are enjoying private time together after the wedding," Ronan said, and disappointment filled her.

"Oh. Their honeymoon."

"Honeymoon?" Ronan asked with a frown. "What are ye on about, lass?"

"Never mind," Kara said, mentally kicking herself. The modern honeymoon didn't exist in this time. She'd have to be careful about what terms she used.

"They'll not be back for some time," Ronan continued after a pause, though suspicion had returned to his expression. "Eadan's left me in charge of the clan and the castle."

"Why aren't you staying there while he's away?" she asked.

"My uncle's retired to his own home; I donnae like spending time at the castle when neither of them are there. The steward tends tae it while me and Eadan are away. Besides," he added, his eyes twinkling with mischief, "I've my own manor tae attend. I need tae protect it from stray lassies wandering the grounds."

Kara couldn't help but smile. She set down her cup, feeling comfortable enough to probe more. And not just to establish trust. She wanted to know more about Ronan.

"Are Eadan and your uncle your only surviving family?"

"Aye. My father died of plague, my mother died when she birthed me. I was broken after my father's death. If it wasnae for Eadan and Bran. . ."

His voice trailed off, sadness filling his eyes, and Kara's heart tightened with sympathy. Centuries may have separated her from Ronan, but they had this in common. Though she'd been young when her mother's death left her orphaned, her life wouldn't have been the same had it not been for Alice's love and guidance.

At the thought of Alice, a renewed determination surged through her. She would solve this mystery for Alice and find her ancestors.

"Are there other villages nearby? Villages where my family may have settled?" she asked.

"There's Mairloch tae the east and Limarty just north of here," Ronan said. "I'll send my messenger tae those villages if ye'd like."

"Yes, I'd like that," she said, hope swelling in her chest.

During the remainder of the meal, he opened up to her more, answering questions about Eadan and his uncle Bran. He told her how Eadan was more like a brother to him, that he'd lay down his life for him, and Eadan would do the same for him. And he told her, though he didn't give her too many details, about a recent illness Bran suffered from, and his fear that he would lose the only father he'd ever known.

"Do ye have any more family?" he asked. "Besides yer grandmother?"

"No," Kara whispered, realizing just how alone she was in her own time. She'd never felt lonely when Alice was alive; her grandmother's love had been more than enough. She lowered her gaze, a wave of sorrow sweeping over her at the thought.

He didn't press her for any more information, but his probing gaze remained on her for the rest of the meal. After they finished eating, Ronan walked her to her chamber.

"I hope ye find yer family while ye're here," he

said, his tone sincere. "And I meant what I said—ye're a guest here, Kara. But I do need tae take precaution."

"I understand."

They both fell silent as his golden eyes held hers. Kara's gaze fell to his mouth, and she wondered what it would feel like pressed against her own mouth. Her throat, her breasts . . .

Desire coiled through every part of her body at the thought, keeping her rooted to the spot. Ronan didn't break eye contact, and it was as the world around her stilled as Ronan leaned forward, his mouth claiming hers in a fervent kiss.

CHAPTER 8

*R*onan plundered the depths of Kara's mouth with his tongue, reaching out to press her beautiful body close to his. The softness of her lips, her curves pressed against him, and her sweet taste consumed his senses.

She reached up to wind her hands through his hair, pressing her body even closer to his, and her hardened nipples pressed against his tunic. She tasted sweet, like cinnamon, and his erection strained painfully against his kilt. He wanted nothing more than to swing the lass up into his arms, carry her into her chamber and bury himself inside her.

But he forced himself to release her, leaving them both breathless as they gazed at each other. Her lips were parted, her chest heaving, her green eyes infused with lust; he made himself take a step back from her, though he desperately wanted to claim her mouth once more.

"I—I bid ye good night," he rasped, forcing himself to turn and walk away.

Though she was more than willing, he would not let himself bed her, not when he didn't know what she was hiding; he didn't fully trust her.

He'd noted her startled reaction when he spoke of Fiona. Did she know her? Were they connected somehow? Until he had some honest answers from her, he needed to keep a clear head around the lass.

Still, he couldn't stop himself from fisting his cock as soon as he was alone in his chamber, imagining his mouth seizing Kara's lovely breasts, tasting the sweetness that seeped from her center, burying himself inside of her, over and over, until they both cried out their release. Ronan gasped and shuddered as he came at the very the thought, sinking back against the wall until his cock deflated.

When he came back to himself, he drew a ragged breath. What was it about her? He'd always been able to control himself around bonnie lasses before. But with Kara, the more he was around her, the more his desire for her grew. And it was more than just desire; he craved to know what was in her thoughts. Who she truly was.

Still aching for Kara, he fell into a fitful sleep, his dreams filled with both images of her and the ill omen of the burnt elder wood tree bark he'd received.

He avoided crossing paths with Kara the next morning, opting instead to ride to Macleay Castle where he took his morning meal. He set himself up in Eadan's study to take care of the day's concerns, trying not to linger on the memory of Kara's body molded to his own, his mouth probing hers. As he worked his way through a stack of land deeds, Osgar, one of Eadan's guards, entered the study.

Ronan stilled, dread creeping through him. Osgar's expression was grim. Something had happened.

"'Tis our lands just south of here," Osgar said. "Lands that belonged to Artagan Graeme, Elspeth's late husband. Someone's burned 'em."

Hours later, Ronan stood in the center of the great hall, the eyes of every noble trained on him. He'd gone with Osgar to take in the burned-down farmlands—the singe marks on the ground indicated someone had purposefully set fire to it. As he'd gazed around at the scorched earth, he realized he could no longer keep what was happening quiet. The burned lands confirmed what he'd feared ever since receiving the ill omen.

Clan Macleay had a new enemy.

"Days ago, I received an ill omen left for me outside my chamber. 'Twas the burnt bark of an elder tree. I hoped there was nothing more tae it, but just today I discovered that someone has taken fire tae our lands," he said, holding the gaze of each noble.

A tense silence filled the great hall; fear and unease crossing the faces of the nobles.

"Has anyone else experienced anything suspicious as of late? Anything that could be deemed a threat?"

There was a lengthy pause until a noble by the name of McFadden spoke up.

"There was a fire in my stables days ago," McFadden said. "I thought—hoped it was an accident."

"And someone left me an ill omen as well," added Uallas, a stocky noble from the northern Macleay lands.

"When I went hunting with my men a few days ago, we thought someone trailed us. Whoever it was, he ran off before we could catch him," said Neasan, another clan noble.

Ronan's dread turned to fear as he listened to several more nobles speak of odd occurrences. On their own, the incidents weren't noteworthy. But added together, it became clear. Someone had indeed targeted Clan Macleay—again. The question was—by whom? And why?

"I know Eadan is off with his new bride," Moireach said, pulling Ronan from his thoughts. "But perhaps we should send a message tae him?"

Ronan stiffened as several of the nobles nodded in agreement. *They don't think me capable as a leader.*

Ignoring the worrisome thought, he stepped forward and drew himself to his full height.

RONAN'S CAPTIVE

"Eadan left me in charge in his stead; I will handle this," he said, his voice firm as he met the eyes of each noble. "And I say we start by questioning the nobles of Clan Acheson. It may just be coincidence that all this has happened after Dughall's defeat—or it may not."

To his relief, no one protested, though he saw doubt in the eyes of several nobles—most notably in Moireach's. A sliver of his own doubt filled him. Perhaps he should send for Eadan.

His thoughts remained a storm of conflict when he returned to his manor. Was his leadership at fault for what was happening? When Dughall targeted the clan, Eadan handled the matter deftly, all the while courting and falling in love with Fiona.

Ronan raked his hand through his hair as he stepped into his chamber. There was a part of him that never felt worthy of his role in the clan, that he was only a high-ranking noble because of Eadan and Bran. What would he be without them? A man without direction, without purpose.

He resisted the urge to seek out Kara, telling his chambermaid he'd like to take supper alone in his chamber.

When a knock sounded at his door, he didn't look up, assuming it was his maid as the door swung open. A dismissal already hovered on his lips when he did look up, but it was Kara who stood there.

"I didn't see you in the dining room for supper," she said, giving him a hesitant smile.

"I—I decided tae dine alone," he said gruffly, averting his eyes. Last night while someone set fire to Macleay lands, he'd been fisting himself as he fantasized about her. He couldn't let her continue to distract him.

"I bid ye good night," he said, keeping his features stoic, his tone polite but curt.

"Good night," she whispered, a flash of hurt in her eyes before she closed the door, leaving him with a pang of longing in her absence. A pang he could not quell.

CHAPTER 9

*K*ara tried to ignore her disappointment as she took her supper alone in her chamber. She reminded herself that she wasn't staying at a quaint bed-and-breakfast with a handsome inn owner; she was the "guest" of a medieval laird who didn't trust her. She had hoped, naively, that after their amazing kiss he'd open up.

Hurt pricked at her chest at the memory of Ronan's cool response when she'd asked him to supper. She'd felt like a schoolgirl whose crush had turned her down to the school dance, not a grown woman on a mission.

There'd been no word from Ronan's messenger about her family's presence in the other nearby villages. So, restless and frustrated, Kara had spent the day exploring the manor. It was even larger than it appeared from the outside, with oak-paneled walls and dark hardwood floors. There were six chambers on the second floor, a massive kitchen in the rear of the manor, alongside several smaller chambers she assumed were servants' quarters, and two drawing rooms, one featuring a massive fireplace. Though Ronan hadn't explicitly forbid her from entering any room, she'd chosen to not enter any of the closed doors on the second floor.

When she'd heard his approaching horse in the evening, she'd been eager to see him . . . until he'd summarily dismissed her.

Remember what you're here for, she told herself now, forcing away her lingering disappointment. *Find your family and get the hell back to your own time where you belong.*

Kara finished her meal with resolve. Aislin, the petite freckled young chambermaid who'd tended to her since she arrived, entered her chamber.

"I can help ye prepare for bed, m'lady," Aislin said.

Kara hesitated to respond. She knew things were different in this time but it made her uncomfortable to have a personal maid waiting hand and foot on her. She'd tried politely refusing her service in the morning, but the poor girl had looked so hurt Kara feared she'd burst into tears.

"All right," Kara said reluctantly, not wanting to hurt her feelings again. "Thank you."

A look of relief flashed across Aislin's face, and she helped Kara disrobe with eagerness. As Aislin moved to a chest at the foot of the bed to retrieve a nightdress, curiosity seized her. If Ronan wasn't going to open up to her, maybe his servants could tell her a little about him.

"How long have you worked here?" Kara asked.

Aislin looked at her with surprise. Kara realized that it was probably uncommon for a "superior" to ask her a personal question. Aislin flushed as she continued to rifle through the chest.

"Almost ten years, mistress," Aislin said politely. Astonishment swirled through Kara's gut; she struggled to keep her face blank. Aislin couldn't have been older than twenty or twenty-one. *You're in 1390*, she reminded herself. Child labor laws were still centuries away.

"And do you like it? I won't tell the laird if you say no," she said with a gentle smile.

"Aye. Very much," Aislin said, her smile genuine as she straightened and stepped forward to hand Kara a nightdress. "He's kind like his cousin and his uncle. Not all lairds are as kind as he. He invited all the servants to share the Christmas feast with him and Laird Macleay at the castle this past winter. If any servant's bairn falls ill he arranges for a healer. Last month, one of the chambermaids grew ill and couldnae work for weeks, but he still paid her wages so her family wouldnae starve."

Surprise and admiration filled Kara and her heart warmed. Not that she expected Ronan to be cruel to his servants, but from what Alice had told her of medieval lairds, his kindness was exceptional.

"And when the laird has visitors," Aislin continued, seeming eager to share word of Ronan's kindness now, "he makes sure they treat us kindly. His cousin and uncle don't need much looking after, but when one of the laird's mistresses—"

Aislin stopped abruptly, her face flaming. Kara forced a smile, ignoring the jealousy that stabbed at her insides.

"It's all right. I'm no mistress of the laird's, just his guest," she forced herself to say, trying not to think of Ronan's lips on hers the night before.

"When he does have—ah—lady visitors," Aislin said, looking hesitant to continue, even as Kara gestured for her to do so, "we rarely tend tae them as they stay in the laird's bedchamber and donnae stay long, certainly not for meals with the laird, as ye have."

Kara's sliver of jealousy turned into a tidal wave. So Ronan was the fourteenth-century equivalent of a playboy. Of course he was. He was handsome, and from the size of this manor, wealthy.

She recalled his mouth against hers, his kiss skilled as he drew a heated response from her. Shame spiraled through her chest. How easily she'd fallen for his charms. She was surprised he hadn't married yet. Or had he?

"Does—does the laird's wife spend any time at the manor?" she asked, her mouth dry.

"Oh, the laird isnae wed," Aislin said with a short laugh, shaking her head. "Are—are ye alright, mistress?" she asked suddenly, her gaze sweeping over Kara's ashen face.

"I'm fine," Kara said quickly, too quickly.

To her relief, Aislin left her alone with a hasty bow, and Kara slipped into bed, trying not to wallow in her ridiculous jealousy. She'd never been the jealous type, always too wrapped up in her work to worry about what her boyfriends were up to when she wasn't around. And now she was jealous over Ronan, a man she wasn't even in a relationship with, whom she'd only just kissed, and who, most importantly, lived centuries in the past.

Get a grip, Kara, she told herself, before falling into a fitful sleep. *You're here for Alice, nothing more.*

THE NEXT MORNING Aislin brought her a tray of food as soon as she woke, telling her that Ronan had left to go to the castle for the day, but wanted her to know she was again free to wander the grounds. Kara pushed aside her disappointment that he'd left; maybe it was better they didn't spend much time together. She needed to focus on what she was here for.

After she ate, she now felt bold enough to open those closed doors on the second floor, and poked her head into each chamber, searching for a study. She hoped to find some records to search through;

records that could potentially contain information about the tenants who lived on Macleay lands.

She located such a chamber at the far end of the hall; there was no bed inside, only a long desk and several cabinets filled with what she hoped were records. But before she could step inside, a male voice behind her made her stop in her tracks.

"The laird's study is off limits, mistress."

She turned as a Highlander right out of central casting approached—tall, burly, and red-haired, dressed in a dark green tunic and belted plaid kilt. This was not the same stocky man who'd guarded her the day before. How many guards did Ronan have on her?

"I'm called Luag," he said, unsmiling, as his gaze swept over her. "I'll be yer guard while ye're here. We'll get along fine, lass, as long as ye donnae wander where ye donnae belong," he added, his gaze shifting meaningfully to the study.

She glared and moved past him. She couldn't bear to return to her stifling chamber, so she made her way to the drawing room, where a young maid practically tripped over herself to start the fire and bring her something to drink, even though Kara insisted she didn't need anything.

But she did appreciate the warmth of the fire after the maid and a male servant started it, a cup of mulled wine in her hands as she sat on a comfortable plush chair, turning to gaze out the window at the manor grounds. The world outside the manor seemed so peaceful. But this wouldn't be the case for long. A portion of Alice's letter entered her mind.

In the spring of 1390, records indicate a fire occurred in the middle of the night during a clan conflict in the Scottish Highlands.

A clan conflict. If she could find out if there was a conflict between Clan Macleay and another clan from Ronan, she'd be a step closer to preventing what would happen next. And she knew of an easy way to get Ronan to tell her what she needed to know—even if he didn't fully trust her.

Good old-fashioned flirting.

Ronan was attracted to her—their kiss proved it. And now that she knew he was a ladies' man . . . she could use the knowledge to her benefit.

"Aislin," she said, when the young maid entered her chamber later that day with her midday meal. "Can you bring me the finest gown you have here? I want to wear it to supper with the laird tonight."

She smiled at Aislin, trying not to think too much about which of Ronan's former mistresses such a gown belonged to.

Aislin looked both intrigued and delighted by her request and left to return only moments later with a deep blue gown with a daringly low-cut bodice.

"Thank you," Kara said, eyeing it. It would serve her purpose well. "This will do."

By the time evening fell, Kara was dressed and

ready. Hearing the clatter of horse hooves in the courtyard, she hurried over to her window, looking out.

Ronan dismounted from his horse, his chestnut waves sexily tousled in the damp evening air. The man seemed to grow more handsome by the day. Kara's breath caught in her throat at the sight of him and she swallowed. *You're supposed to seduce him,* she admonished herself. *Not the other way around.*

She turned to step out of her chamber, taking a breath. It was time for Operation Seduce Ronan.

CHAPTER 10

"My laird," Kara said, her tone demure as she stepped into the entryway to meet Ronan.

Ronan halted mid-stride, taking her in, and there was no mistaking the desire in his eyes as his gaze swept over her.

"I was hoping we could share supper," she continued.

"I—I have matters tae tend," he muttered, starting to step around her, but she blocked his path.

"Please, Ronan," she said, making sure to keep her voice sultry as she reached out to touch his arm. An unexpected rush of warmth coiled through her at the feel of his muscled arm beneath her fingers. "I am your guest, after all."

Ronan hesitated, but finally gave her a curt nod. Relief swept over her. *So far, so good.*

As they settled at the dining room table,

Ronan's eyes trailed from her hair to the swell of her bodice. She tried to act unaffected by his appraisal, but his gaze left a trail of heat down her body.

"Has yer day been well?" he asked.

"Yes," she said. "I was disappointed I couldn't go into your study. I was hoping to find information about—"

"What's in my study isnae yer concern, lass," he interrupted. "I still donnae trust ye."

His words hurt more than they should. She made herself smile, taking a sip of ale.

"Well. I hope to one day earn your trust."

"All ye have tae tell me is what yer hiding, lass."

"I've told you everything."

"Ye're not as good of a liar as ye think ye are," he said, leaning back in his chair to appraise her.

Kara swallowed. This wasn't going to be as easy as she'd hoped. He was far more perceptive than she'd given him credit for.

Ronan turned his focus to his meal, eating in silence.

"You've seemed stressed," she said delicately, hoping she could get him to talk. "For the past day or so. I imagine being the temporary chieftain isn't easy."

"No," he agreed. "'Tis not."

"Maybe I can help."

He gave her a look of disbelief paired with mild suspicion.

"How, lass?"

"I—" she hesitated. She couldn't tell him she used to be an investigative reporter; no such thing existed in this time, and certainly no such job for a woman. "I—I'm good at finding things."

"Finding things?" he echoed, his eyebrows going comically high.

"When something—or someone—went missing in the village where I'm from, the village leaders let me join in the search, even though I'm a woman. It's just something I'm good at. So . . . if there's something you're trying to figure out, I might be able to help you."

Ronan studied her for a long moment, his expression unreadable.

He abruptly got to his feet, approaching her. Surprise coursed through her as he reached down, gently taking her arm and pulling her to her feet.

"What are you—"

"I think," he said, his eyes boring into hers, "that ye're trying tae find out about the clan for yer own purposes."

Damn it. Was she that obvious? She was losing her edge. It had been so much easier to manipulate men in her own time. Ronan and his distracting beauty was too . . . disarming.

"No," she lied. "I—I just want to help."

"And I think, bonnie Kara," he murmured, as if she hadn't spoken at all, "that this lustful gown was meant tae help persuade me. But what ye donnae realize is ye're the loveliest lass I've ever seen, and ye donnae need a special gown to turn my eye."

Kara's mouth went dry as he walked her backward to the wall, still gripping her arm. Once there, he caged her in, placing both hands at the sides of her head.

He reached for her left hand, and she gasped as he placed it against the hardness that swelled beneath his kilt.

"This," he whispered, "has nothing tae do with yer silly attempts at flirtation, lass. That's just at the *sight* of ye. The *scent* of ye. The memory of yer kiss, yer lips on mine, yer body pressed against me. The thought of burying myself between yer thighs and having ye 'til ye scream my name."

Kara couldn't breathe. Her plan had fallen to the wayside. Instead, Ronan's presence consumed her senses—his hot breath on her face, his towering height, his glittering eyes. His lips were only inches from hers, and she was desperate for him to seize her lips. To seize *her*.

His hand dipped to her gown, lifting it up, and her breath hitched in her throat as he pressed a finger into her center, his grin turning wicked at the wetness he found there. He began to slide his finger in and out, in and out, with painful—*torturous*—slowness.

Tendrils of pleasure coiled around her. She reached out, gripping his broad shoulders to hold herself steady.

"Ronan . . . " she said, in a half-whisper, half-moan. He kept up his leisurely pace, and her hands tightened on his shoulders, her gaze locked with his as the tendrils of pleasure tightened around her body, and her orgasm began to build.

"Come for me, lass," he murmured, and her body began to quake, the room twisting and spinning around her as he sped up the pace of his strokes.

"Oh God . . ." she whimpered.

The force of her orgasm roiled through her as Ronan continued to stroke her; she would have collapsed if he didn't reach out to grip her waist with one firm hand.

When she finally stilled, he removed his hand from her center to place his finger in his mouth; the act alone was enough to send another ripple of pleasure through her.

"Yer delicious, lass," he breathed. "As I imagined. But that was just a taste of what I can do tae yer body. When ye finally tell me what ye're hiding and where ye're truly from, then I'll take ye, all of ye," he whispered, leaning forward, so that his lips grazed her ear, nipping at its flesh. "But until then . . ."

He stepped back and gave her a teasing smile before leaving her alone.

Kara closed her eyes, leaning back against the wall, still out of breath. He'd flipped the switch on her and turned her plan on its side. Brilliantly. *Damn him.*

∾

SHE WENT to bed that night with a painful ache between her thighs. Sleep came to her, but it was a restless one, filled with images of Ronan's handsome face, his lips on every part of her skin, her quaking beneath him.

But when she awoke the next morning, a righteous anger replaced her lustful thoughts. Anger—and humiliation. He'd played her body, using her response to him against her. How dare he drive her mad with desire and leave her cold? She'd been as honest with him as she could given the circumstances. She had no desire to get burned at the stake for witchcraft. If Ronan wouldn't tell her what the hell was going on with Clan Macleay, she'd have to take matters into her own hands.

When Aislin came in to help her change, Kara smiled and asked, "Are there any . . . simpler gowns I can wear? The ones I've been wearing are lovely, I just wanted something more . . . more like what you're wearing."

Aislin frowned, a baffled look flashing across her face. She was probably giving the poor girl whiplash. First she asks her for a fancy gown, and now this. She could almost hear Aislin's thoughts: *Why would a lady want to dress like a servant?*

But Kara had a good reason. She wasn't going to sit around this manor all day. She was going to Macleay Castle where Ronan spent most of his days and find out what he was up to. But she needed to blend in—and that meant looking like a servant. The fine lady's gowns she wore wouldn't allow her to fit in.

"Mistress, as guest of the laird, the gowns we've provided are—"

"It would only be for a few hours," Kara said, hoping that her smile was light. "The laird won't even see me in the gown." *I hope,* she added silently.

Aislin looked hesitant, but gave her a reluctant nod, leaving the room. She returned with a simple brown peasant gown.

"This is perfect," Kara said, beaming.

"I'll leave the gown I've brought for ye by the bed," Aislin muttered with a frown.

"I'll change before supper," Kara promised, and that seemed to appease her. Hopefully Aislin wouldn't gossip to the other servants about Kara's odd clothing request.

Kara hurried to the window, looking out. Luag, the burly Highlander who Ronan had guarding her, stood in the courtyard, flirting with a female servant. She took a breath, relieved that he was preoccupied—for the moment.

Ronan's nosy steward, Beathan, usually came in and out of the manor throughout the day; she didn't hear his distinctive brogue ordering the servants around, so she had some time to slip out.

She placed a cloak around her and left the chamber, exiting the rear of the manor. A second guard was usually posted there, but the gods must have been smiling down on her, because he wasn't there today.

She kept her head low as she approached the stables. The stable boy studied her with surprise as she approached, taking in her servant's clothing. She prayed he didn't recognize her as Ronan's guest.

"I need a horse," she said, putting on her best approximation of a Scottish accent. "The laird wants me at the castle. I'm tae work in the castle kitchens today."

She kept her gaze lowered, and to her relief he brought her a horse.

As she mounted the horse, she silently thanked her summers as a camp counselor for her knowledge of how to ride one. And thanks to her long days inside the manor, she'd had plenty of time to watch deliveries from the castle come and go from her window; all she had to do was to follow the next delivery rider east to the castle.

Right on cue, she spotted a servant riding away from the manor, heading due east with a sack hanging off his shoulder. She followed him.

Her heart hammered in her chest as she followed the servant down the winding dirt road east, praying that this last minute plan of hers worked. She soon spotted the castle looming in the distance ahead, and awe filled her chest as she took it in—it was a sprawling castle made of the same gray stone as Ronan's manor, with several turreted towers jutting upward.

She tightened her grip on the reins as she approached, entering the courtyard through the open gate, her head lowered, terrified that a furious Ronan would be on her at any second. When she led the horse to the stables, the stable boy who approached gave her only a cursory glance.

"Are ye here for the spices in the kitchens?" he asked. Kara's heart soared, this was perfect.

"Aye," she murmured, keeping her gaze trained subserviently low.

He gave her a dismissive wave and Kara kept her head bowed low as she made her way into the castle, following two other servants as they entered, carrying a heavy bucket between them. No one in the bustling courtyard paid her no mind, but anxiety clutched her chest until she entered the castle. She expelled a sigh of relief only when she was inside.

Now. How to find Ronan?

Laird's often handled their business in rooms that were the equivalent of studies, or the great hall for larger meetings, Alice once told her.

Kara continued down the long corridor, glancing surreptitiously inside a door that peered into an empty great hall. She bit her lip. She would just have to explore the castle and ask around until she found Ronan. It was risky, but she hadn't come all this way to fail.

"Where is the laird?" she asked a harried-looking chambermaid who walked past her. "I've a message from his steward."

"In the study on the second floor," the maid said, barely giving Kara a glance as she continued down the hall, shouting over her shoulder, "But he's not tae be bothered—he's in a meeting."

A meeting? Perhaps one in which he was discussing a potential clan conflict?

Keeping her head bowed low, Kara made her way down the long corridor and up the first winding set of stairs she came across, hoping that this led to the study. As soon as she reached the second floor, she heard the deep rumble of a familiar voice. Ronan.

With her heart in her throat, Kara made her way down the corridor toward his voice, coming from a chamber at the end of the hall. Two giggling female servants ascended the stairs behind her, and she hurried forward, ducking into an empty chamber next to the study.

She kept the door partially open, straining her ears to listen to the conversation in the next room.

"Is there anyone among the Acheson clan who bears the truce ill will?" Ronan's voice demanded.

"'Tis a large clan; I cannae answer for all. But I will say that most of us are relieved. Not all of us agreed tae Dughall's schemes. Most of us just want peace."

"How can ye explain the threats we've received?"

"I cannae. But I assure ye, 'tis not me nor any of the men I ken—they're all good men."

There was a long pause, and another gruff voice

said, "Or ye can be telling us this because ye're protecting someone."

"I'm not. I'm telling ye the truth, I—"

"I believe ye." Ronan's voice was weary. "If there's anything suspicious ye hear, let me ken."

She heard the door open and the sound of feet retreating down the corridor. Kara held herself still, as Ronan began to speak, but this time she couldn't make out his words.

Suddenly, the chamber door flew open, and a petite elderly woman with blond hair streaked with gray studied her with surprise.

"What are ye doing in here, lass?" she demanded. "This chamber's already been cleaned."

"I—" Kara began, her pulse quickening as she tried to come up with an excuse on the spot.

"And just who are ye?" the woman continued, her eyes narrowing. "I donnae ken ye."

"What is it, Una?"

Kara's heart dropped. The voice belonged to Ronan. The door opened wider, and dread spiraled through her chest as Ronan's startled gaze landed on her.

"Kara?" he demanded, his voice filled with surprise—and anger.

CHAPTER 11

Fury and disbelief swept over Ronan as he gazed down at Kara, dressed in a drab servant's gown.

"Ye ken the lass?" Una asked, turning her gaze to Ronan.

"Aye," Ronan grunted, stepping into the room and glaring at Kara. "Leave us."

With one last suspicious look at Kara, Una obliged. Ronan shut the door behind them, continuing to glower.

Kara took a faltering step back, her green eyes wide, her tongue darting out to lick her dry lips. At the action, an irritating stab of lust pierced him. He'd been furious with her ever since she'd tried to preen for him at supper. Even so, she had looked desirable in that gown, cut just low enough so that he could see the smooth milky white flesh of her breasts. The memory of it had plagued him all day.

"Want tae tell me why ye're hiding in this

castle in peasant's clothes?" he bit out. "How'd ye get out of sight of Beathan? Luag?"

"I can help with whatever you're dealing with," she replied, evading his question. "With—with the clan. I just—"

"So ye thought tae sneak here on yer own? Spy on me?" he demanded.

"If that's what it takes—yes!" Kara snapped.

"Christ, woman, ye drive me mad! Ye'll get back tae the manor and if ye do something like this again, I'll have ye in yer chamber under lock and key!"

"You can't—"

"I can," Ronan snarled. "Ye donnae ken what's happening with the clan, and 'tis best that ye donnae, for yer safety."

"I. Can. Help," she insisted. "If there's some conflict going on, that affects everyone who lives on your lands—including my family. Do you really think I'm going to just sit in that manor like—like one of your mistresses and wait for your messenger to tell me he can't find my family? Do you think I've traveled—that I've come all this way to fail my grandmother? I won't. *I can't.* If I have to disguise myself and follow you to find out what's going on, I'll do it as often as it takes!"

They stood only a hair's breadth away from each other now. Fury and lust battled for dominance as Ronan glared down at her, until lust won the battle. With a frustrated growl, he captured her mouth with his.

Kara gasped into his mouth as his hand went to her breast, kneading it. It was plump and ripe in his hand, and he ached to suckle it.

Kara moaned, returning his kiss with such ferocity that he stumbled back. But she wasn't going to win this battle. He reached out, yanking her body close to his, keeping his mouth latched to hers as he turned, pressing her against the wall.

"Ye make me mad, lass," he whispered, releasing her mouth to suckle the soft flesh of her throat. He kept his gaze locked on her eyes as his mouth lowered to her bodice, nipping and sucking at her flesh, before yanking it down and releasing her breasts from its confines. "Mad with lust. With an ache only ye can fill."

He seized her nipple with his mouth, and she threw her head back, letting out a whimper as he suckled. He wound his hand through her hair, forcing her to look down at him.

"Tell me who ye are, lass," he growled, reluctantly releasing her breast from his mouth. His cock ached to be inside her, and the force of his lust flowed through him, but he held himself still. "Tell me who ye are and I'll give ye what we both want."

Hesitation flared in her eyes, warring with desire.

"All—all right," she whispered, her voice wavering. "But you have to promise me one thing."

"What?" he whispered, lowering his head to pepper her throat with kisses.

"That you'll not have me arrested for witchcraft."

Her words briefly stayed his lust. He looked at her with surprise, but her eyes, even clouded with desire, were serious.

"Kara—"

"Your word, Ronan."

"I donnae believe in witches," he said, and relief flared in her eyes. He leaned forward and again nipped at her throat. "Now. Will ye tell me?"

"Yes," she whimpered. "*After*. I promise. But please—Ronan, I can't wait. I need you to—"

The words were barely past her lips when he knelt down before her, hiking up her gown. She gasped as he lifted her legs, spreading them over his shoulders as she gripped the wall to hold herself steady.

His eyes met hers as his mouth devoured her center, and Kara's hand flew to her mouth to stifle her cry. He took his time feasting on her sweetness, licking and probing her with his tongue, until her body shook and quavered her release.

"Please, Ronan," she gasped, tugging at his hair as he continued to taste her. "Oh God . . . please . . ."

"Please what, lass?" he rasped, removing his mouth from her and lowering her quivering legs to the floor. He stood, stroking his aching cock, his eyes pinned to hers. "Tell me what ye want."

"I want you," she whispered. "I want you to take me."

He obliged her with a growl, sinking his hot member into her center, groaning into her neck at the delicious sensation of her clenched tightly around him. He began to thrust, pounding her against the wall.

It was possible that anyone passing down the corridor could hear them, but he didn't care. In the moment, his entire world was Kara; her soft pliable body against his, her green eyes wild with desire, her quim welcoming him inside of her. Their breath came out in spurts and gasps as they moved together, and Ronan seized her lips as he thrusted. When he tore his mouth away from her, he rasped, "I'm going tae fill ye, lass."

Kara whimpered in response, reaching up to tangle her hands in his air. He leaned forward to suckle the side of her throat, some primal need urging him to brand her. "Take all of me, Kara."

"Yes," she whispered. "Please. . . oh God, Ronan . . ."

It was the sound of his name on her lips that made him come, and he cried out as he spilled his release inside of her. Kara's body trembled against him, and he held her close as her own release claimed every part of her.

When she stilled, he stepped back from her, out of breath. She looked like a seductress, with her gown lowered to reveal her luscious breasts, her hair tousled, her eyes filled with remnant lust. A renewed rush of desire stirred his loins.

"I wish tae make love tae ye properly, in my bed, over many hours," he whispered.

Kara flushed as she straightened her dress. He stepped forward, clutching the sides of her face.

"But first . . . ye gave me yer word. Who are ye, Kara?"

CHAPTER 12

*K*ara made Ronan take her back to Macleay Manor where they could have privacy—and where she could safely drop her bombshell.

Though their lovemaking had left her breathless and reeling, remnant sparks of desire still vibrating beneath her skin, she was able to tell him her story once they were alone in his chamber. Her real story.

And she told him everything. From the year of her birth, over six hundred years in the future, to her grandmother's letter and directive, the pull of wind on her body when she arrived at the ruins of that castle, to her arrival in this time.

She didn't look at him until she finished speaking.

Ronan stood by the window, silent as he looked out at the grounds. His skin had gone ashen; the only indicator of any reaction.

Here it comes, Kara thought with dread—and a stab of hurt. *He'll have his men send me to the dungeons of Macleay Castle.*

But when he turned to look at her, there was no anger. No disbelief. Only . . . comprehension.

"This—village ye came across in yer time," he said slowly. "Describe it."

"There's not much to describe. It was in ruins. It looked like it could be from this time—possibly older," she said, puzzled as to why he wanted to know more about the village.

"Ye said there was a castle? A castle that lay just beyond the ruins of the village?"

"Yes," she said, her heart picking up its pace. "How did you—"

"The village ye went tae in yer own time is called Tairseach," Ronan said. "I've long thought these mere superstitions—but for years there've been rumors of people disappearing around it. Some believe that Tairseach used to be the home of *stiuireadh*—druid witches."

A chill crept down her spine and she took a seat on the edge of the bed. She remembered the line from Alice's letter, about the disappearances in this area.

"I heard a whisper before I disappeared. A woman's voice. She was calling my name," Kara said, unease pooling in her gut. "I thought I was crazy, that it was just the wind. But . . . maybe it was one of those witches."

Ronan grew even more pale and didn't speak for several moments.

"Fiona, Eadan's wife . . ." Ronan murmured, his brow furrowed, "The one with the same accent as yers. Eadan wanted me and his men tae take her tae Tairseach after a battle with another clan—in case anything happened tae him. He still refuses tae tell me where she's really from."

"She's a time traveler as well. She must be," Kara said, shaking her head in a daze. "That was my first thought when you told me about her accent."

"Christ," Ronan muttered, moving to a chair by the window and sinking down into it. "I ken ye were hiding something, but I never expected . . ."

"I swear on my grandmother's grave that what I speak is the truth," she said, approaching him with an imploring look. "I don't know how it's possible—but I've traveled back in time."

"I believe ye, lass," Ronan said.

At the conviction on his face, the tension in her body dissipated, and tears pricked at her eyes. She hadn't realized how important it was that he believe her until this moment—and not just for reasons of self-preservation.

But his face remained turbulent.

"My steward spotted a lass wandering the grounds—a different lass—not long before ye arrived. The night of Eadan's wedding. He claimed tae see her vanish before his eyes, but I didnae believe him. But now that ye're here—from another time . . ."

"Do you think she was a witch? That she had had something to do with my arrival here?" Kara asked.

That whisper she'd heard in her own time. The witch appearing on Ronan's property. The two occurrences could be linked.

"I donnae ken," Ronan said. "'Tis believed the druid witches may have an effect on the disappearances around Tairseach, but no one kens for certain."

Kara bit her lip, her mind whirring. What she wouldn't do for her laptop right now. Whenever she worked on a story, trying to solve the mystery that lay at its heart, she wrote out all her thoughts in a document on her laptop. It made it so much easier to figure out all her unanswered questions when they were laid out before her.

But she wasn't here to solve the mystery of time travel. She was here to save lives.

"You know what I'm here for," she said. "If I can save my ancestors—I can save other lives too. It's why I want to know what's happening with Clan Macleay. Alice found records showing my ancestors' deaths resulted from a clan conflict in this area. Remember how I told you I was good at finding things?" At his nod, she continued, "In my time, I was something called an investigative journalist."

Ronan looked baffled by the term, so she explained the best way she could. "If there was ever a conflict among the nobles of your clan, and you sent someone to find out what happened, how the conflict was started—"

"That would often end in fighting, or a man dead," Ronan said, his eyes filling with worry. "Is that what ye do in yer time, lass? Handle conflicts between men?"

"Not exactly," she hedged. "I answered questions and wrote reports—stories—about the answers I uncovered. And I was good at my job. Finding out *how* something happened doesn't get you killed in the future. At least, not usually," she added, thinking about a couple of dangerous encounters she'd gotten herself into with sources who didn't want her to interview them.

"I'll not have ye putting yerself in any danger," Ronan said with a scowl, reading the shift in her expression.

"Ronan," she said, with an exasperated sigh. "I can help. I *will* help. The only difference is—will you work with me or not?"

Ronan's scowl deepened, but she saw a glint of admiration in his golden eyes.

"Well," he muttered, "I suppose I've no choice."

"No," she said, crossing her arms over her chest. "You don't."

He gave her a grudging smile, and she listened intently as he told her of the former rivalry between Clan Macleay and Clan Acheson, the battle with Dughall, the presumed peace. And the recent threats—fires, thefts, ill omens.

"My cousin left, thinking all was well," Ronan

said, closing his eyes. "But as soon as I'm left in charge . . ."

He looked away from her, but Kara caught the guilt and insecurity lurking in his expression.

"You can't think this is your fault?"

"I donnae ken," Ronan grunted, still not looking at her. "Perhaps this new enemy waited for a weak leader such as myself tae step in for Eadan before they targeted us."

"Or it could have been in the works from the moment your clan defeated Dughall and his men," she returned. "Tell me more about this rivalry with Clan Acheson. What caused it?"

"A land dispute in the north. Long ago, it belonged to their clan. The lands were ceded to our clan generations ago as part of a truce. But the lands are much desired—they're fertile soil in a region where fertile soil is hard tae find. Dughall and others in Clan Acheson believed the lands were still rightfully theirs."

"Who was Clan Acheson allied with?" she asked, mulling over his words.

"They've always worked on their own," he said. "Now they're allied with us. We've purged the members who were on Dughall's side. And I've already considered the possibility of allies. I asked a sympathizer of their clan if they ever mentioned anyone else they were working with; she said they didnae."

"She?" Kara asked, an irrational stab of jealousy pricking at her chest.

"Elspeth. She's a widow in our clan who was close to members of Clan Acheson."

"And do you think she told you the truth?" Kara asked, resisting the urge to demand just how well he knew this widow.

"No," Ronan said with a sigh. "I donnae."

"I think it's unlikely Clan Acheson would have taken on your clan without allies. I think you should keep looking into it."

"Aye?" he asked, his eyes glittering with challenge. "Ye mean tae tell me how tae handle this investigation?"

"I mean to help you," she insisted. "Now you can be stubborn and keep going down the wrong path, or you let me help. I'm from the future, and I know *something's* going to happen that'll cause a lot of innocent people here to die. Unless we do something to stop it."

Ronan's mouth tightened, but he gave her a nod of grudging respect.

"All right," he said. "I'll let ye help. But," he added, his tone firm, "ye may be from another time, but ye're in my time now. I'm laird and leader of this clan in my cousin's stead. Ye must do as I say and stay out of harm's way, do ye understand?"

"Yes."

"And now," he said, advancing toward her, "I have questions of my own."

CHAPTER 13

*R*onan drew closer to Kara, and her mind filled with the memory of his mouth pressed to her center, to her throat, his body flush against hers. A rush of desire coursed through her, and she licked her dry lips. It was difficult to focus when he was so close to her.

"And what is that?" she whispered.

She braced herself for him to ask her what the future was like, what would happen to Scotland, to his clan.

"Is there a man waiting for ye—back in yer own time?"

Raw vulnerability filled his expression, and she blinked at him in astonishment. Out of all the things he could ask, that's what he went with? But delight rippled through her at his obvious jealousy.

"No," she said, smiling. "There's no one."

Stark relief entered his eyes, and he returned

her smile. She stilled as a surge of her own jealousy filled her.

"And you?" she asked, recalling what Aislin told her about his mistresses. "Do you have a mistress or two tucked away somewhere?"

"No," he said immediately. Her shoulders sank with relief. "And now that I've had a taste of ye, lass . . ."

His gaze darkened with lust, and he stepped even closer, encroaching upon her personal space. She met his eyes, heart hammering.

"No other lass compares."

The moment stretched between them, fraught with erotic tension, until Kara couldn't wait any longer. She took the initiative and seized his mouth with hers.

He growled into her mouth as they kissed and they moved in tandem to the bed. As they fell onto it, his hand reached down to lift her gown, his finger dipping into her moist center.

"Ye're already wet for me," he murmured against her mouth. "The first time—that was pure lust. This time," his voice lowered to a husky growl, "'tis for exploration. But first, I need another taste of yer sweetness."

He sat her up as he removed her gown, tunic, and underdress, before lowering her back to the bed and peppering kisses along her abdomen until he reached her center, dipping his tongue inside of her. Kara let out a cry, gripping the sheets as he tasted her. His amber eyes lifted to meet hers, and he tore his mouth from her to whisper, '"The wetness between yer thighs is like the sweetest wine."

"Ronan," she moaned, reaching down for him, aching for him to sink himself inside her, but he evaded her grasp.

"No. I told ye," he said with a wink. "This time, 'tis an exploration."

He kept his mouth on her center until her pleasure reached its climax and she came with a desperate cry. He stood, taking off his tunic and kilt, his eyes roaming her nude body as he did so.

"Christ, Kara," he whispered. "Ye have the body of a goddess."

Kara flushed hot at his compliment, but as she took in his body, all chiseled muscle, every inch of him gleaming and pronounced, she shook her head in amazement.

"And you have the body of a god."

He chuckled, and she sat up, eager to take his hardness in her mouth, but he again pushed her back down.

"All in good time, lass. I want tae savor yer body the way it was meant tae be savored."

He leaned down to seize her nipple in his mouth, laving it with his full attention before turning his focus to the other one. She wound her hand through his chestnut strands, reveling in the feel of him against her, as he bathed her breasts with licks and kisses.

Finally, he lifted himself up, keeping his gaze

locked with hers as he buried himself inside her. Kara wrapped her legs around him, shuddering at the sensation of his length buried within her, and their eyes remained locked as he began to thrust.

Whimpering with pleasure, she lowered her hands to grip his buttocks as he moved within her. Their movements became frenzied, and Kara locked her legs around him, needing him closer as their bodies came together, over and over again, until their mutual pleasure built to a crescendo.

"Kara," Ronan gasped, shuddering as his body quaked with the force of his climax, followed by her own only seconds later, the room swimming around her as her body shook.

Kara struggled to catch her breath as they came back to earth, their bodies still entwined. Rona pulled her close, reaching out to stroke her hair.

"Yer hair is like burnished gold," he whispered, taking her in with reverence. "Yer eyes like the meadows just beyond the manor. Ye are a witch, my Kara, but one of a different kind. Ye've bewitched me since the moment I laid eyes on ye. Do ye know how beautiful ye are?"

"You're beautiful too," she whispered, taking in his tawny eyes, his strong jaw dotted with stubble, those sensual lips, and yet another surge of lust crashed into her.

"If a man said that, I'd spear him with my sword," Ronan said, scowling.

"It's a compliment," she said, rolling her eyes. "You're the most beautiful man I've ever seen."

His eyes darkened. "And how many men have ye seen?"

She grinned. "None have compared to you."

It was true. Even the first kiss she'd shared with Ronan outshone the mediocre sex she'd had with past boyfriends. A sudden pang pierced her. No other man would ever compare to Ronan.

"What is it?" he asked, noticing the change in her expression.

"Nothing," she said, pushing aside the thought of the future, a future in which Ronan didn't exist. "Is there anything else you wanted to know? About my time?"

"No," he said, with surprising swiftness. "'Tis not my place tae ken of the future. But—" he hedged, studying her with curiosity. "Where is this land ye're from? That's given ye and Fiona such a strange accent?"

"Are you sure you want to know?" she teased. "I'll have to tell you a little of the future."

"Aye," he said, "But try not tae divulge much of it."

"There's a land that hasn't been discovered by Europeans yet," she hedged. "People from the countries of Europe will colonize it. After some time has passed, their descendants will speak a common tongue—the form of English I'm speaking now."

"The English," Ronan muttered with an irritated growl. "They still exist in the future, then? The Scots willnae have wiped them out?"

"Yes, I'm afraid so," she said with a rueful grin. She decided it was best to not mention the global dominance England would have in the future—or the fact that Scotland would become a part of the United Kingdom.

"Enough. I donnae want tae ken anymore," Ronan said, his handsome face creasing with annoyance. "But I do want tae ken more about ye, Kara. Not the story ye told me before. The real ye."

Kara rested her head on his chest. "Certain things I told you were true. I was close to my grandmother. She encouraged my love of writing. She was happy that I went into journalism as a profession, though I think a part of her hoped I would've taken more of an interest in history."

She traced the lines of his muscled chest, before continuing, "I immediately started working after university, and I loved it."

"Lasses can attend university in your time?" Ronan asked, his eyes wide with surprise.

"Yes," she said, poking him. "And women can do many other things in my time as well. For years, my life was my work. I didn't get to see Alice as much as I wanted. As much as I should have. I didn't have much time for friends, relationships. Looking back, it's like . . . I was searching for something."

"What were ye searching for?"

"I don't know," she mused. "But I do know that my life felt empty when my job ended. I think . . . I was using my job to fill some kind of gap. I was aimless. And then Alice died . . ." The familiar pull of grief tugged at her, and she swallowed against a wave of tears. "I think that's why I so badly want to do what she asked me to in her letter. This is my last tangible connection to Alice. And then . . . she'll truly be gone."

Her voice broke, and Ronan reached out to pull her into his arms. She buried her face in his neck, the wetness of her tears dampening his skin.

"When I lost my father, I was consumed by grief," he murmured, stroking her hair. "Uncle Bran would take me for long walks in those early days. When we took those walks, he told me tae say everything I wanted tae tell my father, tae pretend he was walking at my side. At first, it seemed mad, but when I started doing it . . . it made his loss bearable. Ye should do the same. Ye'll always have a connection tae yer grandmother. Here," he said, reaching out to touch the center of her chest.

She smiled through her tears, and he wiped away her tears with his thumb, his eyes soft with compassion.

Alice may be gone, and she was six hundred years in the past, but in this moment, for the first time in a long time, a sense of calm settled over her. A sense of home.

CHAPTER 14

*R*onan remained awake long after Kara drifted off to sleep in his arms. He gazed down at her sleeping form, ruminating over her story. As soon as she told him she was from another time, as strange and unbelievable as it was . . . it made sense. The vagueness of her backstory. Her strange accent. Tairseach. The stiuireadh who'd shown up on his property before she'd arrived.

And there were the similarities to Fiona. Fiona had shown up in a similar manner, emerging from the cellar of Macleay Castle in a scandalous dress, one that must be common in their time. Her accent, nearly the same as Kara's. Eadan's refusal to tell him Fiona's true place of birth.

Fiona had traveled through time. Just like Kara.

Why hadn't Eadan told him the truth about his wife? Did he not trust him?

But as Ronan studied Kara, reaching out to

brush a stray lock of hair back from her face, a surge of protectiveness filled him—and he understood. Eadan wanted to protect his wife. Though Eadan and Ronan weren't superstitious, there were many in the castle and surrounding villages who were. Many fervently believed in—and despised— witches. And they would certainly consider a lass who could travel through time a witch.

He now understood with stark clarity why Kara hadn't wanted to reveal who she was, and guilt flooded him. For all she knew, he could have thrown her into the dungeons and had her hung for witchcraft.

"I'm sorry, Kara," he murmured to her sleeping form. She was here on behalf of the grandmother she adored, and he'd not made things easy for her.

A sudden heaviness settled over him. Since Kara didn't belong in this time . . . her stay here would only be temporary. Soon, his Kara, with her spirited mind and fierce heart, would return to her own time. He'd never wanted a lass by his side for more than a few weeks, but with Kara, the thought of her leaving filled him with a sharp ache.

He drifted off to sleep with the troublesome thoughts of Kara's eventual departure, and awoke from his fitful sleep at first light, kissing Kara's fore- head before extricating himself from her warm, beautiful body with reluctance. Her suggestion of continuing to look into Clan Acheson's potential allies was a good one; he would broach it during the meeting with the nobles today.

Even though he was allowing her to help, he'd have to keep her out of sight of the clan nobles. The only people aware of her presence here were his servants and his men, but they were loyal and wouldn't gossip about his mysterious guest to outsiders. If the clan nobles knew of her existence, they'd have questions—and suspicions. It was a miracle Fiona had passed muster. He didn't know if Kara would be so fortunate.

Once dressed, he stepped out into the hall. He intercepted Aislin as she made her way to Kara's chamber.

"The lady is asleep in my chamber," he said. "But let her rest."

"Aye, m'laird," Aislin said, averting her gaze, but he saw the delight in her eyes. Aislin must have taken a liking to Kara and seemed pleased that she'd spent the night in his bed. *I plan tae keep her in my bed,* Ronan said silently, as Aislin moved past him. *As long as I can.*

He descended the stairs with a small smile curving his lips. At the sight of Beathan approaching him, Ronan's smile vanished. He was going to have words with him and Luag about allowing Kara to slip from the manor.

But Ronan froze at the taut look of worry on Beathan's face.

"M'laird, a messenger just sent word," Beathan said, "the men who watch Elspeth's manor stopped by for their morning check, and they found her gone. She's fled."

~

Ronan dismounted from his horse, his heart thundering in his chest as he approached Elspeth's manor. Osgar stood in the courtyard, standing opposite a frightened-looking chambermaid.

"Was Elspeth taken by force?" Ronan asked when he reached them.

"No," Osgar said, his mouth set in a grim line. "I've already searched the manor. It looks like she packed before she left."

"Did she say anything? Tell ye she may go somewhere?" Ronan asked, turning his focus to the chambermaid.

"No, m'laird," the chambermaid said, shaking her head. "But last night after she took her supper, she dismissed me before I could help her tae bed. Me and all the other servants. Said she wasnae feeling well and wanted tae be alone."

"Did she seem ill?"

"She seemed fine, m'laird."

Dread filled Ronan's chest, and he stepped into the manor. He recalled Elspeth's evasiveness the last time he was here. He was a fool to not have kept a closer watch on her.

Another chambermaid led him to Elspeth's chamber, which confirmed what Osgar told him—her clothing chest was empty, along with a box of jewels. This wasn't someone who'd been forced to leave.

Where did she go? Was she now working with the same person sending threats to the clan?

"Send men to the surrounding villages, and search the roads," Ronan told Osgar when he returned to the first floor, though he doubted they would find her. If she'd left the night before, she was long gone by now.

He made his way to the castle, where the nobles were gathered in the great hall for the meeting.

Tension coursed through Ronan as he told them of Elspeth's abrupt departure.

"I already have men searching for her," Ronan said. "I'm hoping we'll find her before she gets far."

He braced himself for their accusations—that he should have known Elspeth was planning something given her closeness to Clan Acheson, that he should have kept a closer watch on her with Eadan gone.

Moireach and the nobles leveled him with hard gazes, but the great hall remained silent until McFadden spoke up.

"'Tis not Elspeth we're concerned with," McFadden said, studying him with narrowed eyes. "'Tis the foreign lass ye have in yer manor."

Ronan stiffened. How did they know about Kara? Was someone watching his manor—or had one of his trusted servants gossiped?

"My manservant saw ye with her yesterday," McFadden continued, as if reading his thoughts. "He overheard her strange accent as ye left the castle with her. He said it looked like ye didnae want tae be seen. I had him follow ye back tae yer manor."

"I am leader of this clan, McFadden. Ye had no right tae have yer man follow me," Ronan growled. "The lass is my mistress. I donnae see how she's any of yer concern."

If they thought she was a mere mistress of his, Ronan hoped they'd drop the matter. But their eyes narrowed with even more suspicion.

"And when did this lass arrive?" Uallas pressed.

"Days ago," Ronan replied tightly.

"And ye donnae think 'tis odd that as soon as this lass arrives, our clan starts receiving threats?" McFadden demanded.

"We've received threats before she came here," Ronan snapped, trying not to show his alarm. He didn't want their suspicions trained on his Kara.

"It would be a good way of distracting ye," Neasan spoke up. "Send a bonnie lass yer way for ye tae bed while Eadan is away—"

"And what are ye trying tae say, Neasan?" Ronan hissed. "We're all grown men. No need tae dance around it."

"Eadan wouldnae let himself get distracted. Even with the Sassenach he ended up marrying, he still kept his focus on Dughall and saved our clan. Ye've been chasing anything with skirts yer entire life, and now this whore shows up—"

Ronan lunged toward Neasan. Osgar darted in front of him, holding up his hands.

"M'laird," he said, turning to give Neasan a hard look. "I'm sure Neasan didnae mean what he said."

"I'm sure he didnae," Ronan said, through clenched teeth. "Am I right?"

"My apologies," Neasan said, though his tone was not at all apologetic. "But 'tis our right tae question her."

"No," Ronan growled.

"No?"

"No," Ronan repeated, firm. "She's my mistress; ye've never needed tae question any mistress of a clan noble before."

"We questioned Eadan's wife," McFadden interjected.

"Kara's not my wife," he returned, an odd ache piercing him at the words. "She's my mistress, and she has nothing tae do with any of this. We need tae focus on who is after us, not on who I'm bedding. We need tae talk tae more members of the—"

"We've already spoken to a dozen of Clan Acheson's nobles," Uallas interrupted.

"We've been asking the wrong questions. I donnae believe 'tis the Acheson clan sending us threats—Eadan executed the treasonous ones. This may be an ally of the Acheson's, someone who wants tae claim the disputed lands."

"And how do ye ken?" Neasan asked, his eyes narrowed with suspicion.

"'Tis a reasonable guess," Ronan said. He wouldn't dare suggest it was Kara's idea. "We need tae do everything we can tae find out who this is and what they're planning. These threats—ill omens and such—they seem like mere distractions. I fear something more dangerous is about tae happen."

"I TOLD YE, I wasnae keen tae Dughall's conversations," Seamus said. "He kent I didnae agree with his plans."

Ronan stood in Eadan's study opposite Seamus, a member of Clan Acheson who'd once been close to Dughall. He'd questioned several men from Clan Acheson since his meeting earlier that day with the nobles, and they'd all sworn ignorance about potential allies.

"Do ye ken if Dughall or any of his men had allies?" he asked. He expected Seamus to answer the way the others had—that he knew nothing.

But Seamus stiffened.

"What?" Ronan asked, hope surging through his chest. "What do ye ken?"

"'Tis is only a rumor," Seamus hedged, "but I heard Dughall had several meetings with the chieftain of Clan Sudrach months ago. It was thought nothing came of it."

Ronan studied him, excitement replacing his hope. No one had mentioned such meetings before.

He thanked Seamus and dismissed him, sinking down into his chair. He didn't know much about Clan Sudrach, they were a northern clan that stayed out of conflicts and kept to themselves. But if Dughall met with them months before he launched an attack on Clan Macleay . . .

Had he discovered Clan Macleay's new enemy? Was Clan Sudrach behind the renewed threats?

CHAPTER 15

*W*hen Kara awoke to find herself alone, anger and irritation coursed through her. She'd told Ronan the truth; he'd agreed to let her help, and he'd still left her alone to sit like a useless statue in his manor.

Aislin entered with a fresh gown and tunic for her to change into. Her face warmed as she realized that Aislin probably gleaned what happened between her and Ronan the night before. But the smile Aislin gave her was neutral—and there was a hint of satisfaction in her eyes.

"Do you know where the laird is off to?" Kara asked, hoping she didn't sound too needy.

"I assume he went tae the castle," Aislin said, looking surprised by Kara's inquiry. Kara could detect the silent question in her eyes: Ronan goes to the castle on a daily basis. Why would today be any different?

Because he knows who I am. We made love last night. I opened up to him, and he opened up to me.

Her mind still humming with frustrated thoughts, Kara made her way to the study once Aislin left her alone. This time Luag didn't stop her, and she flipped through records that looked like land deeds, but there was no mention of a Suibhne or Orla.

It was midday when she set down the last deed, rubbing her eyes. How thoroughly had Ronan's messenger checked the village for her family? Alice had told her that the most important records about each village's residents were kept in its church. If she could go to the village church and take a look at the records herself, perhaps there was something there that Ronan's messenger had overlooked.

Kara found Luag in the courtyard, flirting with a different young female servant. He stiffened as she approached, regarding her with wary appraisal.

"M'lady," he said with forced politeness, giving her a curt nod.

"I'm going to the village," she said, hating that she had to ask permission. She reminded herself that an unaccompanied woman wasn't common—or safe—in this time. "I assume Ronan wouldn't want me to go unaccompanied."

"The laird gave ye his permission tae go?"

I don't need his permission, damn it.

"Yes," she lied. "He—wants me to check something for him. At the church."

Luag still looked uncertain.

"I'll go on my own if I have to," Kara said with impatience.

Luag glowered at her; he understood her meaning. She'd snuck off to the castle just the day before.

"All right. But ye stay close tae me."

Moments later, Luag rode alongside her as they headed to the nearest village, which Luag told her was a few miles south of Ronan's manor.

A sense of awe flowed through her when they arrived at the village. *Alice would have loved this,* Kara thought, taking it in. Thatch-roofed cottages, winding dirt streets, taverns, workshops, villagers wandering to and fro. The pungent scent of butchered meats, the shouts of merchants hawking their wares. It was times like these that it hit her she was truly in another time.

Kara tried not to stare too much as they entered the village, but other than her sojourn to Macleay Castle, this was the first time she'd ventured out of Ronan's manor to see the outside world as it was in 1390.

They soon arrived at the church, a small steepled building in the center of the village. Luag tied their horses to a nearby post and accompanied her inside. A short portly man who looked like a clergyman approached, his eyes straying to Kara with curiosity.

"Luag," said the clergyman with a broad smile. "Did the laird need something?"

"He wants me to review the church records,"

Kara said, stepping forward. "He's . . . looking for someone."

The clergyman's eyes widened—not only at her strange accent, Kara guessed, but over the fact that she could read. He looked to Luag, who gave him a curt nod.

The clergyman turned, entering a back room and returning with a records book. He handed it to Kara, his eyes narrowing as she sat down in a pew to flip through it.

To her relief, Luag stepped forward and engaged him in conversation as she read. The clergyman's wide-eyed stare would have made it difficult to concentrate.

The records book had logged baptisms, weddings, tithes—along with names. But there was no Suibhne and Orla listed.

Defeat roiled through her chest, and she thanked the clergyman before she and Luag left to ride back to the manor.

Your ancestors are here somewhere, she reassured herself, through her cloud of disappointment. *You'll find them.*

She felt Luag's curious gaze on her face as they rode, and she glanced over at him. He looked away, training his attention on the dirt road ahead. She didn't know how much Ronan had told him about her, and curiosity lurked in his eyes.

"Thank you for accompanying me," she said. "How long have you been working for Ron—for the laird?"

"A long time," he said, and there was a trace of warning in his eyes as he continued, "Long enough tae be loyal."

His meaning was clear. He didn't trust her, and he had every intention of telling Ronan about their little outing. She pressed her lips together and turned her attention back to the road. So much for her attempt to be friendly. They rode back to the manor in silence.

But there was no need for Luag to tattle. As soon as she dismounted from her horse, a furious Ronan strode out of the manor. She let out a startled cry as he gripped her arm and practically dragged her inside, just as he had the first day she'd arrived in this time.

Once they were alone in his chamber, he glowered down at her, his tawny eyes infused with anger. Even when enraged, he was ridiculously beautiful, and a heated awareness coursed through her body.

"I ken things are different in yer time," he hissed, his voice low, "but in this time ye donnae leave whenever ye like. There are—"

"Your man accompanied me," Kara snapped, fury flooding her. So he *was* going to keep treating her like a captive, even though he'd agreed to let her help. "And I just went to the village. I wanted to search the church records—see if I could find my family's names there."

"My men are trusted in the village, as am I. If they say yer family isnae in the village, ye must trust their word. Kara, things—things have grown more dangerous. I donnae ken what's happening, but 'tis not safe for ye. The nobles ken about ye, and they're suspicious. 'Tis best ye not leave the manor. At least, not without me."

"Ronan— "

"Ye gave me yer word last night," he said, his voice growing husky, and an image of his mouth on her skin filled her mind. She swallowed, as he continued, "That ye'd do as I commanded."

Kara gritted her teeth. She had agreed to that, damn it.

"Fine," she snapped. "*But*—I want. to be included. I'm not going to sit in this manor doing nothing. I told you, I'm good at what I do. It would be foolish not to use me to help."

"Ye can—within reason. I had tae leave in haste today because Elspeth has fled Macleay lands."

"Elspeth," Kara echoed, struggling to recall the name. "The widow? The one who was close to Clan Acheson?"

"Aye," he said grimly. "We're searching but I fear she's long gone. I can only pray she just fled tae make a new life for herself, and not tae another clan tae work against us. I've arranged tae talk tae the chief of another clan tomorrow," he continued. "It seems Dughall may have made an alliance with a clan to the north, Clan Sudrach."

Kara stilled, her heart leaping into her throat. Could this be it? The soon-to-be-deadly conflict Alice had mentioned in her letter?

"Ye were right," he admitted. "Dughall may have had allies."

"Ah," she said with a grin. "Say that again, Ronan?"

His eyes glittered, but his lips twitched with amusement. "I said ye were right, Kara."

"Again."

"Kara—"

"Ye were right. I willnae say it again, lass."

"I'm coming with you. To talk to this chieftain."

The amusement vanished from his expression.

"No."

"I won't say a word—I'll stay silent. Please, Ronan," she said, hating that she had to resort to begging. "You've already taken one piece of my advice and found useful information. Imagine how much more I can help."

"Fine," he grunted, his mouth tight. "But ye'll remain silent and ye'll not protest when I give ye orders."

"You have my word," Kara said, relief coursing through her.

"I'm sorry if I was harsh with ye—about going tae the village," he said after a pause, his expression softening. "When I returned and didnae find ye here—I was a feared something had happened tae ye."

Kara's heart leapt at his concern. Did he feel something more for her than just desire? *Not that it matters,* she told herself, but the admonishment didn't stop the delight that rippled through her chest.

"I understand," she murmured. "I'll be careful. I'm not used to the way things are here. In my time, women have more freedom."

"I can tell," Ronan said wryly, stepping forward. He reached out, grazing her lip with his thumb, and she stilled, her heart picking up its pace. "Ye're not like any lass I've kent, Kara. Witch," he said with a wink.

A charge of erotic heat spiraled through her as he continued to stroke her lip with his thumb. He walked with her backward to the bed, lowering his thumb to her bodice, over the swell of her breasts, lower . . .

Kara moaned, and Ronan gave her a wicked grin.

"Ye may want tae press yer hand over yer mouth, witch," he whispered. "We donnae want the servants tae hear yer screams."

CHAPTER 16

As soon as Ronan woke the next morning, he wanted to take back his agreement of having Kara accompany him to see the chieftain of Clan Sudrach. He didn't know what to expect at the meeting. What if he and his men were met with violence? To make his visit seem as neutral as possible, he was only bringing two men with him—Osgar and Luag. How could he protect her?

Kara woke just after him, giving him a smile that made her look even more lovely as she sat up. She studied his tense expression and stiffened, as if sensing his hesitation.

"Do we leave now?" she asked, slipping out of bed and covering her luscious curves with nightdress. She turned to face him, her green eyes flashing with challenge, as if daring him to go back on his word.

Ronan's body ached with tumult and desire as he took her in. She was a vision of loveliness, her golden hair tousled, the sleeves of her nightdress slipping to reveal the fine curve of her shoulders. He'd kissed those shoulders the night before as he'd pounded into her, burying his face in the softness of her strands. The memory made his cock harden, and he turned away from her, swallowing hard.

"Aye," he said curtly. It would do no good to convince her to stay behind. Knowing Kara, she'd follow him anyway. "But I meant what I said Kara. Ye're tae be silent. If ye donnae obey, I'll have ye sent back here."

"And I gave you my word," Kara said, her lips tightening into a thin line. "I won't do anything foolish. I just want to help."

"Good," he said, approaching her, his gaze sweeping down to the high bodice of her night dress. He already regretted what he was going to say, but if she was to come with him, it was necessary. "My first order starts with what you're going tae wear tae this meeting."

"And what is that?" Kara asked, giving him a wary look.

Moments later, Kara stepped out the front door of the manor wearing the gown he'd ordered Aislin to dress her in. It was a daring gown the color of crimson, the bodice cut low. A jolt of desire darted through him—along with a ripple of jealousy. He wanted the chieftain to think Kara was a low-born mistress of his, someone he didn't care for and was merely with him to sate his lust, and she needed to dress the part.

But now he doubted his own plan as he saw just how desirable she looked in the gown. He didn't want the chieftain—or any man—to look at his Kara, his witch, with desire in that sinful gown.

"I think I understand what the plan is," Kara said with a sigh, adjusting her bodice as he took her hand and led her to waiting carriage. "Wait. You don't want me to . . . seduce anyone, do you?"

The jealousy that struck him at her words hit him with such force that he yanked her against his body, not caring who was watching.

"Never," he hissed. "Ye're tae stay at my side, silent as a frightened animal, do ye understand? I hate that any other man gets tae gaze upon yer loveliness, but I need him tae think ye mean nothing tae me, that ye're just a body tae warm my bed. But we both know ye're more than that."

It was more than he wanted to confess, but it was true. He didn't want to think about the day when she left his side to return to her own time. Kara's eyes flared with emotion and she nodded, looking away from him.

They were silent during the carriage ride north; Kara's quickened breathing and clenched hands revealed her tension, tension that matched his own. He gazed out the window at the surroundings to calm himself. He rarely ventured to this part of the Highlands, spending most of his time at the castle and the lands around his manor; Eadan was the one who made lengthier trips for diplomatic talks with other clan leaders. At the thought of his cousin, uncertainty pierced him. This was the first diplomatic meeting he attended on his own. *Ye can handle it,* he reassured himself, though doubt clouded his mind.

Kara seemed to sense his edginess, reaching out to lace her fingers through his, giving him a reassuring smile. He returned it. He hadn't realized how comforting her presence was until now.

The carriage soon arrived at a lone castle that stood out among the craggy, dark green hills that surrounded it.

"Wow," Kara whispered at his side. "It looks like the lair of a villain right out of a horror movie."

He turned to her with a puzzled frown.

"Movie?" he echoed. "Wow?"

"Wow is a term of surprise," she said, her lips twitching. "As for the word movie . . . that requires more explanation. I'll have to tell you later."

A rush of warmth coursed through him at the image of Kara in his bed later, explaining some of her strange words from the future. The thought comforted him; it was something to look forward to after they took care of this unpleasant business with Clan Sudrach.

"I'm just trying to say this castle doesn't look like it's the home of the nicest person in the world," Kara continued.

He returned her amused smile and followed her gaze to the castle. Castles were meant to appear foreboding; they were fortresses built to keep intruders out, but this one did seem particularly sinister. But his amusement faded as their carriage made its way to the gate house.

"Remember what I said," he said, his expression turning firm. "Ye're tae stay silent, and if I tell ye tae get back tae the carriage ye'll do so."

"I will," she promised, giving him a firm nod.

They arrived in the small circular courtyard and stepped out, where several rough-looking clansmen greeted them. They gave him, Luag and Osgar curt nods, their appraising and lustful gazes then sweeping to Kara. He moved to stand in front of her, blocking her from their view, and their eyes glinted with annoyance as they turned, leading them down a long corridor and into a massive great hall.

In the largest chair in the center of the hall, a chair that resembled a throne, sat a tall, broad-shouldered man with cruel silver eyes and long dark hair streaked with gray. This was Tarag, chief of Clan Sudrach.

Ronan abruptly froze. Not at the sight of the man, but at the dark-haired woman who sat at his side.

It was Elspeth.

CHAPTER 17

*E*lspeth gave him a cool smile edged with defiance. A searing hot rage filled Ronan, and he clenched his fists at his sides. Damn it, had she been working with Clad Sudrach the entire time?

"Ronan of Clan Macleay," Tarag said, his tone sharp and unfriendly, "I donnae believe I've met ye. I've met yer cousin once. Eadan. Could he not join us?"

Ronan's gaze was still fixed on Elspeth, who evenly returned it. She shifted her eyes to Kara and stiffened.

"Ah, I see ye and Elspeth ken each other," Tarag said, looking not at all perturbed that Ronan hadn't answered his question, his eyes shifting back and forth between Elspeth and Ronan with sly amusement.

Ye ken we're acquainted, ye bastard, Ronan

thought. He'd been in the room for mere seconds with the man and he already hated him.

"She's a member of Clan Macleay," Ronan said, still leveling her with a hard stare. "She vanished from her manor and we've been concerned as tae her whereabouts."

"I'm no longer the concern of Clan Macleay," Elspeth snapped. She reached out to take Tarag's hand. "I'm tired of yer clan treating me like a prisoner though I've done nothing wrong. My husband has been dead for some time; I want tae move on with my life but none in yer clan will have me. Tarag has proposed; I'm tae be his bride."

In exchange for what? Alarm skittered through Ronan but he tried to keep his expression neutral.

"Congratulations," he said past stiff lips. "I wish ye would have informed us before ye chose tae depart so hastily."

"My movements were restricted. Ye never would have let me leave," Elspeth spat.

"Elspeth—"

"Ye can address any concerns ye have about my future bride tae me," Tarag interrupted, the amusement gone from his expression now. "Ye didnae answer my question. Where is the chieftain of yer clan?"

"He is away with his new bride. I'm serving as chief in his stead," Ronan said, finally looking away from Elspeth to Tarag.

"Ah," Tarag said. "Tae a foreign lass, I hear. A Sassenach. None in my clan would marry one not from these lands. We ken not tae trust foreigners—especially a Sassenach."

His eyes drifted behind him, and Ronan's dread rose as his silver eyes landed on Kara. But fury replaced his dread at the lust that filled Tarag's eyes. Though Ronan couldn't see Kara, he sensed her tension at Tarag's appraisal.

"And who is this bonnie lass?"

"My mistress," Ronan said, trying to make his tone as dismissive as possible. "Sometimes she travels with me."

Elspeth stilled at Tarag's side, the jealousy in her eyes plain. Disbelief struck Ronan. Is this why she'd turned to Tarag? Did she hope to gain his attention by her betrayal?

"She is bonnie," Tarag mused, his eyes lingering on Kara. "'Tis been some time since I've had a lass with hair the color of sunshine. There's no need tae be jealous, Elspeth," he added, as Elspeth scowled.

"I've come here tae discuss an important matter," Ronan said. He wanted to turn the conversation away from Kara; he didn't know what he'd do if Tarag kept looking at her with lust in his eyes. "I wish tae offer ye and yer clan an alliance. As ye know, Clan Acheson and Clan Macleay have put their differences aside. Together, perhaps we can form a sept."

It was an idea he'd come up with the night before; he needed a good reason for his hasty visit. He didn't want Tarag to know of his suspicions about his clan. Offering a truce seemed the best way to glean information from the chieftain.

"I've never had a problem with either of yer clans," Tarag said with a dismissive wave of his hand. "Why would I need tae ally?"

"It could be tae our benefit. In case a rival clan ever wanted tae stake a claim on any of our lands. We could band together for joint protection."

There was a long moment of silence as Tarag seemed to consider this, pressing the tips of his fingers together.

"I thank ye for yer offer," he said finally. "But my clan is fine on its own. Unless," he continued, a wicked smile curving his lips, his silver gaze flickering to Kara, "ye've something tae trade."

The quiet fury that stirred beneath Ronan's skin erupted. His hand flew to the hilt of his sword, as Tarag continued, "Even just a night with the golden lassie in my bed would be worth a—"

Ronan charged toward Tarag, ignoring the warning shouts of Osgar and Luag.

Tarag's guards instantly surrounded him, their hands going to the hilts of their swords. Elspeth stumbled back, her hand flying to her chest.

Osgar and Luag came to Ronan's side, their hands going to their own swords.

Ronan took several heaving breaths to calm himself. It would be foolish to start a battle with Tarag in his own castle when he was so outnumbered. But Ronan ached to sink his blade into

Tarag's chest for even looking at Kara the way he did.

"'Tis all right."

He stiffened as Kara stepped forward with a seductive smile, and both surprise and anger roiled through him as she made her way to his side. The look she gave him said, *trust me.*

Panic swirled through his veins, but he remained still. *What the hell are ye doing, Kara?*

"Ronan can be a wee bit jealous, but he's shared me in the past. I'm a mere lassie, not worthy of such a trade for an alliance."

Ronan stood stock-still, his heart hammering. Kara's Scottish accent was impressive—it was only slightly off, and he was grateful she'd used it instead of her natural one. That would have invited far too many questions—and suspicion.

Tarag's eyes widened, and he barked out a laugh.

"Apologies. I thought ye were a foreign lass," he said, his eyes roaming up and down her body, filling Ronan with even more fury.

"'Tis an honest mistake. I'll wait for ye in the carriage, Ronan. The matters ye discuss here donnae concern me."

With a respectful bow to Tarag, Kara left the hall.

Ronan watched her go in quiet disbelief—and grudging respect. Somehow, her words had eased the tension in the room; all the men had relaxed, and some had looks of amusement in their eyes.

"Ye share that seductress?" Tarag asked, shaking his head in disbelief. "I'd not want tae let anyone else between her thighs. But she's right. Even a lassie as sweet as her is not worth Clan Sudrach becoming entangled with other clans. I've no wish tae ally; my clan stands fine on its own. As such," he continued, his tone hardening as he got to his feet. "I donnae appreciate ye and yer men nearly attacking me in my own castle. If ye donnae leave now . . . I cannae promise I willnae retaliate."

"You two were about to kill each other," Kara said as their carriage raced away from the castle moments later.

Ronan sat in silence, his fingers pressed to his throbbing temple. Not only had he not gotten any information from Tarag, he'd almost started a battle in the man's castle.

Kara had taken his silent tension for anger and defended herself as soon as he stepped into the carriage.

"I had to do something," she continued. "I had to make it seem like I was a bottom-level mistress, someone you wouldn't mind sharing under different circumstances. Someone you didn't care for. It seemed the only way to diffuse the tension."

"I'm not angry with ye, lass," he muttered, dropping his hand from his temple to look at her. "I'm angry with myself. I almost attacked him because of petty jealousy. I hated the way he was looking at ye. And when he mentioned having ye in his bed . . ." He trailed off, clenching his fists at the memory. "But 'tis no matter how I felt. I should've controlled myself. 'Tis what good leaders do."

Kara reached out to take his hand.

"You are a good leader," she insisted. She hesitated, before continuing, "Elspeth seemed . . . upset that we were together. She looked like she wanted to kill me. Were you lovers?"

An unmistakable flare of jealousy shone in her eyes. Ronan pulled her close into the crook of his arm.

"We kissed once, but that's as far as it went. I suspect she wanted more, but I never felt anything for her," he said. "Nothing like the fire that spreads through my belly whenever ye're near, witch."

Kara flushed, the jealousy vanishing from her eyes as she smiled.

"Do you think that's why she joined Tarag?" she asked, her smile fading. "Because she wanted you, and—"

"No," he said. "'Tis more than about me. I think Elspeth's a lonely lass; she's been lonely for some time. Many in the clan are suspicious of her; she doesnae have many companions. She likely feels no loyalty to Clan Macleay. I think Tarag offered her the attention and companionship she craves. Which is why," he continued grimly, "I think that Tarag is behind the threats. With Elspeth at his side, he kens what our weaknesses are. 'Tis just a matter of getting proof that 'tis him."

Kara nodded, her expression troubled. He didn't want to tell her that he also suspected, despite Kara's performance, that Tarag had to know by Ronan's violent reaction to his "offer" of taking Kara, just how important Kara was to him.

It was knowledge that Tarag could use against him—and that scared Ronan more than any other threat Tarag could direct at the clan.

CHAPTER 18

*T*he encounter with Tarag plagued Kara's thoughts during the journey back to the manor. There was something dark about the man, something that unsettled her to her core. She'd once written an article about a man on death row for a double murder, and she'd seen the same savage cruelty in his eyes that she'd seen in Tarag's.

Revulsion had roiled through her when Tarag looked at her with lust. She could see a man like Tarag easily murdering anyone who got in his away, even innocent bystanders like her ancestors.

At her side, Ronan remained quiet for the rest of their journey, and when they arrived at the manor, he remained in the carriage, telling her he needed to head to the castle.

"I have tae tell the nobles about Tarag—I cannae take ye with me, Kara," he added, with a look of apology. "They think ye're just a mistress, and 'tis best they keep thinking that."

She nodded in reluctant agreement; she was still too shaken over the Tarag encounter to protest. She stepped back, watching as the carriage rode away from the manor.

WHEN RONAN RETURNED HOURS LATER, he told her the nobles agreed to have Tarag and his men followed until they had proof that he was indeed behind the threats.

"And when they do have proof?" Kara asked.

"We'll have tae fight," Ronan said, his face tight with anxiety. "And I'll have no choice but tae call my cousin home."

For the first time in days they didn't make love that night. Ronan held her as she tried to drift off to sleep, worried thoughts racing through her mind. What if they couldn't stop Tarag before he put a plan into place, a plan that included the fire that would kill her ancestors and other innocents? What if she was already too late to stop him?

Kara hoped that Ronan's spies would quickly find proof that Tarag and his men were behind the threats, but over the course of the next few days, Ronan told her they reported nothing out of the ordinary. Tarag, it seemed, rarely left his castle, and his men remained close to their lands, never venturing south. And the threats to Clan Macleay had ceased.

The days seemed to become stuck in a holding pattern. Ronan would leave at first light to head to the castle where he tended to matters of the castle and the clan, all the while keeping track of his men's progress with Tarag. Kara would spend her days trying to locate her family, reading every single deed in Ronan's study, along with the ones he brought back with him from the castle. But none of the deeds mentioned the names of her ancestors, and for the first time she started to wonder if Alice's information was wrong. Perhaps her family hadn't died in this time.

But instinct told her that wasn't the case. Alice was a detailed historical researcher; she wouldn't have had Kara go back in time with faulty information.

When Kara wasn't buried in land deeds, she found that she'd settled into the fourteenth-century with surprising ease. She usually hated wearing dresses—her go-to outfit in her own time was jeans and a comfortable T-shirt, but now she found herself enjoying the comfortable loose tunics and gowns she wore on a daily basis. The food didn't taste as bland as Alice had described; while it wasn't as rich, it was still flavorful, and one of her favorite meals became one the cook served often: vegetable stew thickened with bread, roasted chicken with a sweet wine imported from France.

She also grew used to the relative peace, quiet, and beauty of the Scottish Highlands, a panacea to modern New York City's constant hubbub. She even came to enjoy the manor, which at first seemed unnecessarily large and imposing, and spent a lot of time in the drawing room sitting by the fire on cool evening nights.

And she did live better in this time than she had in her own. A tiny apartment in Brooklyn didn't compare to a Scottish manor full of servants and your own personal chambermaid . . . not to mention a handsome laird.

Despite the relative luxury of her surroundings, she had to admit that it was Ronan's presence that helped her settle into this time most of all. But it was her growing feelings for him that caused her the most conflict.

She missed Ronan while he worked at the castle; she'd rush to the window at the sound of his horse's hooves approaching the manor, a ripple of joy coursing through her at the sight of him. She relished their suppers together in the dining room; as soon as the conversation shifted from Tarag and Ronan's investigation, they discussed Kara's job in the present day, Alice, and snippets of how life was in the future, as Ronan didn't want to know too much. Ronan would tell her details of growing up with Eadan, the trouble they'd get themselves into, the feasts at the castle, the silly disputes he'd gotten into with fellow clan members during his younger years before he'd matured.

She avoided acknowledging the true depths of her feelings for Ronan until one rainy afternoon.

She'd been at the manor for almost a month, weeks since they'd met with Tarag, and she was making her way past the kitchens to Ronan's study when she overheard her name on Aislin's lips.

"—'Tis the longest the laird has kept a mistress here," Aislin said.

"He'll not marry her," the voice replied; Kara recognized it as the voice of the cook, Greer.

"And how do ye ken?" Aislin asked. "I like the mistress. She's kind."

"I'm sure she is. But I overheard him talking with Luag. He told him he's keeping her around because 'tis a novel experience, the experience between the thighs of a foreign lass."

"Ye ken ye shouldnae speak of the lady in such a manner!" Aislin snapped, sounding genuinely offended on her behalf.

Kara hurried away, entering Ronan's study and closing the door behind her, tears stinging her eyes. Ronan could have told Luag those things in order to maintain the façade that she was just a mistress he didn't care much for. *Or he could have meant every word,* she thought bitterly.

Even if he did mean what he'd said—what did it matter? It wasn't like she'd stay in this time and marry him. Once they handled this business with Tarag they'd go their separate ways.

The pain that gripped her chest at the thought was so severe for a moment Kara couldn't breathe. She imagined living her days in the present, Ronan long dead, the memory of him soon fading into nothing but an impression. She thought of his tawny eyes, the low rumble of his laughter, the warmth of his embrace, his determination to take on the mantle of leadership in his cousin's absence. And the realization struck her.

She loved Ronan. It was a foreign feeling—she'd never been in love before, not even close—but if this was what all those love songs had described, she felt it in spades. That rush that went through her every time she laid eyes on him. The warmth that lingered in every part of her after they made love. The need to know his every thought, to mean more to him than just a body he desired. The yawning chasm of emptiness that filled her heart when she thought of her life without him in the future.

Kara swallowed, and a multitude of emotions surged through her: guilt, panic, anxiety. She was here to save the lives of her ancestors, to fulfill Alice's wish—not to fall in love. And she'd still not made any significant progress on that task, other than locating the man likely responsible for their murder. All she'd done in this time was fall in love with a man, one who didn't even exist in her own time, one who didn't share her feelings.

"Are ye all right, lass?"

Kara whirled, blinking back tears as Ronan stepped into the study, his brow furrowed with concern. He looked handsome as always; his chestnut hair dampened by the rain, his beautiful eyes trained on hers with worry.

"I'm—fine," she hedged, forcing a smile. *I just realized I'm in love with you, fourteenth-century Highlander. No big deal.*

"I donnae think that's true, Kara," he said gently, crossing the room until he stood only a hair's breadth away from her.

"I'm—just frustrated by my lack of progress," she said, hoping a half-truth would satisfy him. There was no way she'd confess her love for him. Ronan was a playboy, probably used to his mistresses falling in love with him; she doubted she was the first. She needed to return to her twenty-first century self, the Kara who focused only on the job. That Kara would have never allowed herself to fall in love on the job, unlike this misty-eyed, love-struck Kara. She could push these feelings aside, bury them while she solved Alice's mystery, and when she returned to her own time, they would dissipate. They would.

"There's something else that's bothering ye," Ronan pressed. "Yer eyes betray ye, lass."

He already knew her too well. Perhaps that was one of the reason she loved him—he read her better than any other man could.

"I overheard the servants gossiping," she said, deciding to bite the bullet. "About how you're only keeping me around because . . . because of the experience you have in between my thighs."

"Ah," Ronan said after a pause, his mouth twitching in amusement. "I remember saying that."

"I didn't realize it was so funny," Kara said stiffly.

"Kara, I told him that tae make it seem like ye're not important tae me," Ronan said with slight exasperation. "'Tis the same thing I wanted Tarag tae believe. And a part of it is true."

Kara scowled, hurt pricking at her spine, but Ronan stepped forward to cup her face in his.

"A part," Ronan insisted. "Ye must ken I care for ye, lass."

Care. Did she really expect him to confess his love? Kara forced a smile.

"All right," she said. "Not that it matters."

"Aye?" he asked. "If it didnae matter, then why did ye seem upset?"

"Pride," she lied. "And it doesn't matter because I'm only here temporarily. Soon I'll be back in my own time."

Something flickered in his eyes, and his amusement faded.

"Ye're right," he said, but he kept her face cupped in his hands. "I ken ye're only here briefly, but with all that's been happening . . . I've missed ye. I will miss ye."

His eyes darkened with desire, and Kara's mouth went dry. She should tell him they needed to stop making love, that they needed to focus on their mutual goal.

"I've been in your bed many nights," she said instead, lowering her gaze as heat stained her cheeks.

"Not enough, lass," he returned. "Not nearly enough."

She was powerless to stop the rush of love and desire that flowed through her as his lips crashed onto hers. He swung her up into his arms to carry her to his chamber. She may not have a future with him, but she could enjoy the time she did have.

So she allowed herself to live in the moment, to let her body express the words she wouldn't say, stripping him of his kilt and tunic.

He watched her, breathless, as she pushed him down to the bed and took him in her mouth, licking and stroking the length of him with her tongue until he came with a shudder. She swallowed his release, keeping her eyes locked on his burning ones.

"Christ, Kara," he groaned, rolling her beneath him and burying himself inside her with a pleasured moan.

He began to thrust, leaning down to seize her breasts with his mouth, laving them with his tongue. From her chest to her core, desire spiraled through her.

"Come for me, witch," Ronan panted. "Come for me, my Kara."

The pleasure in Kara's body climbed to a climax, and she obliged, her body shaking and trembling as he continued to thrust, burying his face in her neck as he cried out his own release.

Kara wound her hands through his hair as he

stilled, keeping her eyes closed, as if preventing him from seeing her love in their depths.

I love you, Ronan.

❧

THE NEXT DAY, Kara entered Ronan's study just after first light, determined to put her game face back on and shove her feelings for Ronan aside.

But after reading the millionth deed, she set down the parchment and rubbed her bleary eyes, tired of not making any progress.

When one path isn't working, take another path. It was a personal motto she'd recited whenever she couldn't solve a problem for a story she was working on. Her reviewing land deeds, Ronan sending his spies to follow Tarag—none of it was working. They needed to try something else before it was too late.

She stilled as an idea seized her. It was risky and dangerous, but it was something. And it couldn't wait. She needed to tell Ronan, now.

She headed downstairs to find Luag to escort her to the castle. But as soon as she stepped into the entryway, the door flew open, and she stumbled back with a yelp.

Three Highlanders entered, glaring down at her. Both Beathan and Luag darted out of the drawing room and hurried to her side, Luag shoving her behind him.

"What is the meaning of this?" he demanded, glaring at the men. "Does Ronan ken ye're here?"

"He doesnae need tae know," one of the men growled, advancing toward her.

She stumbled back as Luag took a challenging step forward. The man ignored him, keeping his dark gaze trained on Kara.

"Ye're going tae tell us who ye really are, lass. Without Ronan here tae protect ye."

CHAPTER 19

*R*onan gazed out the window at the bustling castle grounds. The sky was gray, the air thick with the promise of a storm. The weather was fitting; the relative peace they'd experienced over the past few weeks seemed like the calm before the storm.

There had been no incidents, no acts of aggression toward Clan Macleay since his and Kara's visit to Tarag. Though he'd received word from one of his spies that Tarag had wed Elspeth, the man himself had not left the grounds of his castle, nor were there any suspicious movements from Tarag's men.

But none of this eased Ronan's anxiety. Each day he feared receiving word that someone had burned more of their lands—or worse, that people had been killed, just as Kara's letter from her grandmother had spelled out.

And then there was the matter of his witch, his

Kara, who occupied every corner of his mind. Kara wasn't like other lasses, and not just because she was from the future. There was her beauty—her luscious body that fit so perfectly to his own as he explored her in his bed. But there was also her fierce mind, her determination, and even her damned stubbornness that he admired. His heart ached at the loss it would suffer when she left this time. When she left him.

He tried not to dwell on her eventual departure from his life. He would savor his time with Kara, as scarce as it was these days.

"M'laird."

Ronan turned. Moireach stood at his doorway, his face tight with tension. Ronan stiffened, waiting for Moireach to scold him about some castle business he'd handled incorrectly in Eadan's absence.

But no such admonishment came.

"I thought ye'd want tae ken—McFadden and two other nobles have gone tae yer manor. They intend tae question yer . . . guest. I overheard them discussing it."

Fear clawed its way through Ronan's chest. He gave Moireach a grateful nod and rushed out of the study.

Luag is with her, he reassured himself moments later, as he raced away from the castle at a frantic pace, tightening his grip on the reins. *He'll not let them harm her.*

He raced back to the manor, urging his horse to gallop faster than he'd ever made him go, dread coiling around him at the thought of the nobles interrogating Kara without him there. Kara was smart and capable, but what if they threatened her? What if they ordered her imprisoned until Eadan returned?

He arrived at the manor to find the door open, and as he stumbled inside he heard raised voices coming from the drawing room. One of them was Kara's.

He darted into the dining room, his hand already flying to the hilt of his sword.

Kara stood opposite McFadden, Uallas and Neasan, glaring at them while Beathan and Luag stood protectively before her. They all turned as he entered, and Kara's face filled with stark relief.

"What are ye doing in my manor?" Ronan growled, moving to stand next to Luag, shielding Kara from their gazes. "If ye're threatening a lass that belongs tae me—"

"If yer lass is a spy, we've every right tae question her," McFadden returned. "Ye've let her bewitch ye. We've another clan after us, and we need tae—"

"My cousin left me in charge while he's away; ye take yer orders from me. And I ordered ye tae leave her be," Ronan snapped.

"It's all right."

He turned with surprise at Kara's calm voice. She hadn't attempted a Scottish accent this time, and the nobles' eyes widened. She gave Ronan a shaky but reassuring smile, stepping past him and Luag.

"Kara—" Ronan began.

"There's no need to fight among ourselves when there's an actual enemy out there, and I don't want to be the cause. I can assuage their fears by answering their questions."

Moments later, Ronan stood at Kara's side as she sat at the dining room table opposite the suspicious clan nobles. He'd dismissed Beathan and Luag; it was just the five of them now.

She'd told them the same story she'd initially told him; she was here on her grandmother's behest seeking out her family. She did add that she was a relative of Fiona's, which Ronan thought was wise, given the similarity of their accents.

Ronan told them he'd offered her his manor to stay while she searched. His eyes flashed with challenge when McFadden tried to inquire about the details of their personal relationship.

"'Tis not yer business. We've told ye what ye want tae ken," Ronan snapped.

"How do we ken ye speak the truth?" Uallas asked, eyes narrowed, turning his focus to Kara. "That ye're not trying to seduce the laird tae help Clan Sudrach?"

"You don't," Kara said calmly. "I want to help because my family lives somewhere on your clan's lands. You're just going to have to trust me. Before you barged in here, I'd just come up with a plan. A plan I think will help prove Tarag is the one working against your clan."

"Even if we believe ye're not working against us, that doesnae mean we'll include ye in clan business," McFadden snapped.

"I gave her permission tae help. It was her suggestion tae keep looking for allies Dughall may have had," Ronan spoke up.

"'Tis not acceptable," Uallas growled, shaking his head. "A lass isnae fit tae give advice tae—"

"You listen to me," Kara interrupted, leaning forward to glare at him. "Your clan is in danger. At this point, you should take good advice from wherever you can get it."

"And what is this advice?" Neasan demanded.

"That we go directly to the enemy to find out what they're planning. They know your men are watching them. That's why they're not doing anything incriminating," Kara said.

"We tried that," Ronan interjected with a frown.

"Not Tarag himself," Kara said. "One of his men. One of his *susceptible* men. And you shouldn't use one of your spies to uncover this information. You use a woman. Me. I can find out information in ways that only a woman can."

The room fell silent as her meaning settled in. The nobles looked both scandalized and intrigued while a dark wave of disbelief and jealousy swept over Ronan.

"No," he barked. "This meeting's over."

"Ronan—" Kara began.

"This meeting is over," he repeated. "Ye've questioned her, and I assume her answers have satisfied ye. Now go."

"The lass may be on tae something," Uallas hedged. "If she—"

"Get out of my manor. That's an order," Ronan hissed.

The nobles obliged with great reluctance, casting Kara looks of growing admiration before they left.

"Are ye mad?" he asked, turning to Kara when they were alone. "Tae even suggest—do ye ken how dangerous that would be? What they'd do tae ye if ye were found out? Tarag kens how important ye are tae me. I willnae allow it."

"I wouldn't actually *sleep* with one of his men," Kara said with a look of revulsion. Relief filled him, his jealousy abating. "I've done other things to get men to open up when working on a story in my own time. Flirt. Seduce in other ways."

"Flirt? Seduce?" Ronan roared, his jealousy returning. "Ye didnae tell me this profession of yers entailed behaving like a harlot."

"Flirting is harmless," Kara said through gritted teeth. "And when the stakes are this high—when *lives* are at stake—"

"No," Ronan barked, advancing toward her. "I'll not allow ye tae give yer body tae another."

"I just told you—I wouldn't actually sleep with anyone! I would just talk. And—and just because we make love doesn't make me your property! We both know what I'm really here for."

"Ye do belong tae me," Ronan snapped, as Kara got to her feet, glowering at him. "And aye, I do ken what ye're here for. But while ye're here in my time, with me inside ye every night, ye'll not 'flirt' or 'seduce' anyone. Do ye understand?"

He could tell she was trying to maintain her defiance, but the desire in her eyes was winning. He maneuvered her to the table, leaning forward to graze her ear with his lips, reaching down to stroke the flesh between her breasts.

"The craving that's spiraling in yer belly?" he whispered. His own desire coiled in his gut, and he hardened beneath his kilt. Kara's breathing had quickened, her lips parting as she met his eyes. "That proves ye belong tae me. There will be no seducing of Tarag's men—or *any* man."

RONAN HOPED Kara would calm down and understand why he wouldn't go along with her foolish and dangerous plan, but she barely spoke to him the next morning, only offering him her cheek when he kissed her goodbye before heading to the castle, although they'd made passionate love the night before.

As she turned away from him, a rush of anger filled him. She wasn't from his time and didn't understand the dangers, damn it. Fear gnawed at his gut at the thought of what Tarag would do to her if he caught her. If her anger was the price he had to pay for her safety, so be it.

At the castle, he presided over another meeting with his nobles. To his relief, McFadden, Uallas and Neasan seemed to no longer hold suspicions about Kara now that they'd questioned her. There was no news to report; Tarag and his men had made no movements out of the ordinary, and no one in the clan had reported any more threats.

"Yer lass's idea may be a sound one," McFadden said gruffly, approaching him after the meeting was over and the other nobles had left. "We need tae take the offensive rather than waiting for Tarag tae act."

"No. 'Tis too dangerous," Ronan said, glowering at him.

"I thought she was just a mistress ye were bedding," McFadden said, surveying him with mild suspicion. "If she was yer wife, I wouldnae dream of suggesting—"

"It doesnae matter that we're not wed. She's not involved in this."

McFadden studied him for a long moment, his mouth tight, looking as if he were on the verge of protest. He finally turned and left the great hall.

Ronan drew in a sharp breath, wishing there was someone he could confide in about this. Usually that person was Eadan. But . . . there was one person he could talk to.

As evening fell over the countryside, he rode his horse to his Uncle Bran's home. He found Bran in the drawing room, sitting by the fire.

Bran looked flushed and healthy, and relief flowed through him at the sight. Weeks before, Eadan and Fiona had discovered that Dughall was having him poisoned. He'd recovered well.

Bran turned as Ronan entered, delight flaring in his eyes at the sight of his nephew.

"Ronan," he said, starting to get to his feet, but Ronan gestured for him to remain seated as he took the chair opposite him. "What brings ye here tae visit an old man?"

Ronan hesitated. He didn't want to involve his elderly uncle in what was happening with the clan now that he'd retired from clan business. But he needed advice.

So he told Bran everything that had happened since Eadan's wedding. The only thing he left out was Kara's status as a time traveler, though he wondered if Bran knew about Fiona.

Bran remained silent for a long moment when Ronan had finished, his eyes thoughtful.

"Ye're not going tae like my opinion, but yer lass is right. The best way tae get information out of a man is through a bonnie lass."

Ronan scowled. "'Tis dangerous, I'll not— "

"Being a leader means making sacrifices. If ye trust ye and yer men tae protect her, there's no reason ye shouldnae try her plan," Bran said.

His expression shifted and he suddenly leaned back in his chair, giving Ronan an appraising look.

"Ah. I see what's happening here."

"What?"

"I think," Bran said, his eyes twinkling, "that what I told ye at Eadan's wedding has come tae pass. Ye've met the lass who has changed everything for ye."

CHAPTER 20

*K*ara forced down a piece of roasted chicken; Ronan hadn't come home for supper and she was dining alone in her chamber. That was probably for the best; she was angry with him over his pigheaded refusal to go along with her plan. She hated the feeling of uselessness, the sense that she was twiddling her thumbs while a disaster loomed.

Beneath her anger over his rejection of her plan was a sliver of hurt. She loved him and wanted him to have faith in her resourcefulness, to prove that she could be more than just a warm body in his bed. That she could be . . . more to him.

She blinked back a sting of tears, turning when she heard footsteps approach the doorway. Ronan stood there, the tumult on his face plain as he stared at her. Hot awareness seized her; she hated that just the sight of him affected her so much, even when she was angry with him.

He entered the chamber as she set down her knife, stopping when he stood opposite her.

"I spoke to my uncle," Ronan said, raking his hand through his hair. "He thinks yer plan is a good one. It seems yer plan is quite popular."

"That's because it can work," Kara said, hope filling her chest. "Ronan, please consider—"

"We'll do it," he interrupted. "We'll carry out yer plan."

Kara leapt to her feet with a cry of delight, flinging herself into his arms. He held her for a moment before pulling back.

"But we must take every precaution. Ye ken how dangerous this is," he warned.

"I know," she said, her heart hammering with anticipation. "But I think this will work, Ronan."

He nodded, but his eyes shadowed as he reached down to grip her hands, lifting them to his lips to kiss.

"I just—I worry, lass," he whispered. "Ye . . . ye mean more to me than any mistress I've had."

The words should have warmed her heart; instead a shard of jealousy pierced her at the comparison to other mistresses. It was far from a confession of love.

"And you mean a lot to me," she said, lowering her gaze, not wanting him to see what an understatement her words were. "Now . . . let's go get the sons of bitches who are after your clan."

Ronan's eyes widened, and he chuckled with amusement.

"Aye," he said. "We shall."

THE NEXT NIGHT, Kara rode her horse alongside Luag through the darkened countryside, approaching the tiny village of Orridon, several miles north of Ronan's manor.

She adjusted the gown she wore, the same blue gown she'd worn when she'd attempted to seduce Ronan for information, her heart pounding in her chest.

Think of this as just another assignment, she told herself, to slow down her racing heart. *If the assignment were over six hundred years in the past and lives were at stake.*

It had been a busy day. Ronan allowed her to accompany him to the castle where they'd learned from one of his spies that Tarag's men frequented a tavern in Orridon, on the outskirts of Clan Sudrach's lands.

They'd decided that Kara would go to this tavern with Luag, who would pose as her brother; travelers just passing through the Highlands. Ronan had provided her with descriptions of several men she should focus on, advising her sternly to only pick one. While Luag ordered their food and drink, she would flirt with Tarag's man, getting as much useful information out of him as possible.

Before they'd left the castle, Ronan gave her a

dagger that now lay stashed beneath the sleeve of her gown; she was to use it in case things went south. Kara hoped she wouldn't have to use it. She'd never used a weapon on anyone in her life, even during a couple of hairy instances in her own time.

Orridon loomed up ahead, a quaint medieval village filled with brick and stone buildings, thatch-roofed cottages and winding dirt roads, mostly empty at this hour.

Kara cast a quick glance behind them. Somewhere in the distance, Ronan and his men trailed them. They would lurk outside the tavern, entering only if Luag and Kara ran into trouble.

Luag gave her a look as their horses entered the village, as if to ask, *are you ready for this?* He'd regarded her with grudging respect ever since she'd suggested this plan; she wondered if her bold plan had won him over.

She gave him a quick nod and dismounted from her horse when they reached the tavern, taking several deep, steadying breaths as he tied up their horses and they headed inside the tavern.

As they entered, Kara took it in. Alice hadn't told her much about medieval taverns and ale houses. This one didn't look too different from a dive bar in the twenty-first century—small, dark, and filled with drunken men. To her surprise, there were a handful of women; two were with male companions, and one worked at the bar.

When she and Luag entered, all eyes fell on her

with several of the men giving her appreciative looks.

Well, there goes the first part of my plan. While she wanted to attract the attention of Tarag's men, she didn't want to attract *too* much attention.

Trying not to show her anxiety, Kara simply gave the men a flirtatious smile. She wanted to give off the air of a "wanton" woman of loose morals for this time, not a prim noblewoman, even though she wore a fine gown.

She scanned the tavern and spotted one of the men Ronan had described. He was short and balding, with a small scar curving from the side of his mouth. *Here goes nothing.*

She and Luag took the table next to the man. Luag gave her a brief but meaningful look as he stood, leaving her alone to get them drinks. The man's eyes landed on hers, lighting up with lust, and she gave him a flirtatious smile.

"I'm called James," he said, his voice slurred. "Ye're a bonnie lass." He jerked his head toward Luag, who was purposefully taking his time ordering their drinks. "Yer husband?"

Kara's smile widened. He was drunk—as they'd hoped. It would be easier to coax and manipulate him. And he could hopefully overlook her terrible Scottish accent.

"I'm Caren," she said. "And no, he's not my husband. My brother."

"Aye?" he asked, licking his lips. She ignored the revulsion that roiled through her at the act.

"Aye," she said with a wink. "My brother's trying tae find us safe passage for the night. We've heard rumors of a clan feud in these lands."

She tried to make herself look both worried and demure; knitting her brows together in a frown. James straightened, practically puffing out his chest, giving him the look of an overblown peacock.

"Well, lass," he said. "Ye're safe with me."

He glanced over to where Luag now stood conversing with the barkeep and scooted his chair closer to hers, draping his arm over the back of her chair. She bit back her disgust, forcing a smile as he leaned forward, his musky breath filling her nostrils.

"Why? Is there no dispute? I heard rumors about fires on Macleay lands, and ill omens being sent to the nobles," Kara said.

"'Tis a farce," James said, waving his hand with dismissal. "A mere distraction."

Kara stiffened, hoping she didn't look too surprised.

"A farce?" she pressed.

The door to the tavern suddenly swung open, and Kara froze as Ronan entered the bar with two of his men. What the hell was he doing? He wasn't known in this village, but they'd decided it was best he kept out of sight just in case someone recognized him. He didn't look their way, but his jaw was tight as he and his men headed to the bar.

Damn it, Ronan. I love you, but I'm going to kill you if you screw up this plan.

James followed her gaze, but she reached out to touch his face, forcing his attention back on her.

"Farce?" she repeated.

"Aye. Ye have nothing tae worry about, lass," he slurred, leaning forward to kiss her.

She jerked back, noticing out of the corner of her eye that Ronan had turned to face them, and Luag had reached out to hold him still.

"Perhaps—perhaps we should go somewhere private," she said, swallowing.

She hated the thought of being alone with this leech, but she didn't think Ronan would keep it together if James tried to kiss her again. This was a part of her plan she'd hoped to not have to undertake. Plan B. Once she got him to talk, she was to get a drink from the bar and spike it with opium that one of Ronan's men had given her, a small jar of which was now tucked in her bodice. The drink would put him into a deep sleep and she could then slip out of his room.

"Aye," James said, stumbling to his feet with an eagerness he didn't try to disguise. "I've a room."

Kara forced another smile, taking his elbow as they made their way to the stairs in the corner of the tavern. She gave Ronan a sharp look and recoiled from the barely contained fury she saw in his eyes.

What was his problem? This was just part of the plan.

She returned her focus to James as they

climbed the stairs and made their way to a tiny room at the end of the hall.

As soon as they entered, James pressed her against the wall, but she slipped out of his grip.

"I cannae relax if I donnae feel safe," she said, looking at him with what she hoped was a flirtatious smile. "What do ye mean, a farce?"

"Our chieftain doesnae care about Clan Macleay," James said, his eyes pinned to her cleavage. "He only wants the lands Dughall wanted—their lands in the north. While Clan Macleay scrambles tae put out fires and frets over ill omens, he's putting men in the north tae claim their lands for Clan Sudrach. So there's nothing tae worry about, lass. Now give me that sweet—"

Before he could finish his sentence, the door swung open and a furious Ronan charged past her, striking James in the head with the hilt of his sword.

CHAPTER 21

*R*onan glared down at the unconscious man, his sword burning in his grip, aching for him to stir. At his side, Kara's hand flew to her mouth.

"Ronan, what the hell was that for? I was going to—"

"I couldnae bear ye being in this room with another man," he growled. "Come with me. I'm going tae act like yer my wayward mistress and I'm jealous—which I'll not have tae feign."

Though Ronan and his men were supposed to wait outside the tavern, his fear for Kara had grown so great he'd ignored the protests of his men to stalk into the tavern. He'd come close to charging the bastard Kara flirted with when he'd tried to kiss her, and when she'd led him upstairs Luag had to restrain Ronan from racing after them. He trusted Kara and knew she only wanted to get information, but the lass didn't know just how desirable she was.

171

He'd barely contained himself when she turned her charms on him.

Ronan's fists tightened as he continued to glare down at the man; the bastard was fortunate he hadn't done more damage.

"Did he kiss ye again? Touch ye in any way?"

"No," Kara snapped, and his jealousy calmed— somewhat. "I was handling this, Ronan. He was giving me information. *Useful* information. You told me you trusted me to— "

"It's him I donnae trust," he snapped. "Now come."

He marched with her out of the room and down the stairs, Kara glowering at him as they went. The other patrons watched with amusement —he wondered if scenes like this were common occurrences at the tavern.

As they rode back to his manor, Ronan made himself steady his breathing. He'd never felt such jealousy before; while he'd agreed to Kara's plan, he'd underestimated the force of his jealousy.

He slid a sideways glance at her; she gripped the reins of her horse, a scowl darkening her features, looking gorgeous as sin in her blue gown. He was going to have Aislin burn it when they returned to the manor.

He dismissed his men as soon as they arrived at the manor, informing them he'd meet with them at the castle at first light to go over what he'd learned from Kara.

"You owe me an apology," Kara snapped, when

they entered his chamber. "For not trusting me to handle myself back there. Once you hear what I've learned, you're going to kick yourself. It's information we can use."

"Kick myself?" He frowned at the strange phrase. "Why would I do that?"

"It's a common phrase we use in my time. It means you're going to regret what you did," she snapped.

"I thought I could handle my jealousy, but I couldnae. Ye're mine. How would ye have felt if I had to seduce a lass for information?"

Kara's scowl deepened, a murderous glint in her eyes.

"So ye see how I felt," he said, his lips twitching with amusement. "Now, I hope ye *have* learned something of importance, because I willnae let ye do something like that again."

"He said the attacks on your clan are all a farce," Kara said.

Ronan froze as she told him that the threats—the fires, the ill omens—were all a distraction while Tarag and his clan claimed their lands in the north.

Ronan closed his eyes, understanding now why she was so angry with him. She'd learned information that changed everything.

"I thank ye, Kara," he said, reaching out to grip her hand. "And ye have my apology. I acted like a jealous fool. I donnae ken we'd have found that out on our own—at least not until it was too late."

"Apology accepted," Kara said with a conciliatory smile as she squeezed his hand. "And thank you for going through with my plan, even though I know it was hard for you." She studied his face, worry infusing her expression. "What are you going to do?"

"I've a plan of my own."

RONAN SLEPT LITTLE THAT NIGHT, getting out of bed to pace the dark halls as Kara slept. He would send for Eadan at first light; his plan involved many men of their clan, and not just clan nobles. By the time his message reached Eadan, he'd already have carried out his plan. It would end with their lands safe and Ronan alive, or it would end with their lands lost and Ronan dead.

He paused outside the door to his chamber, looking in at Kara. She slept on her back, her golden hair spread around her like a halo, the moonlight filtering in through the window illuminating her lovely features.

He'd told her the details of his plan, but he'd left out one thing. His desire for her to go to Tairseach and return to her own time. He knew Kara would push back—she still hadn't found her family. But he believed her grandmother would want her safety above all else.

An ache pained him at the thought of losing her—through his death or by the expanse of time.

He recalled his uncle's words. *Ye've met the lass who's changed everything for ye.*

Ronan couldn't deny his uncle's words. She had changed everything for him. He no longer feared the responsibility of a family, a bride—as long as the bride was Kara. And if there was no danger, and she was from his time, he'd have no hesitation in asking her to be his bride. To live out her days at his side, as his lady, to make his cold empty manor into a home with her bright, shining presence. She'd embedded herself in his heart, in every part of him.

But that was why he'd let her go. He loved her enough to prioritize her safety from Tarag and his clan, to send her back to the time where she belonged, even though his life would be empty without her. Even though he loved her.

"I love ye, my time-traveling witch. My goddess," he whispered to her sleeping form when he slipped back into bed, curling his body around her.

He'd just fallen asleep when a sharp knock sounded at the door. It was barely first light; the light outside the windows still dim.

Ronan sat up, his body heavy with fatigue as he padded to the door, swinging it open. Beathan stood there, beaming.

"Eadan has returned," Beathan said. "He's in yer drawing room."

~

Moments later, Ronan stood opposite Eadan, while Kara sat in a chair in the corner.

He'd told Eadan everything—the threats, Elspeth's defection, the meeting with Tarag, and Kara's recent discovery that it was all a distraction to seize their lands. Kara had told him of the latter, describing her encounter with Tarag's man at the tavern, and Eadan had stiffened in surprise at her accent. But Ronan told him with his eyes an explanation for that would have to wait—there were more urgent matters to handle.

Now, he waited tensely for Eadan to scold him, to tell him he should have sent for him sooner, that he'd take over from here.

"This plan of yers," Eadan said. "What is it?"

Ronan blinked with astonishment. His cousin didn't look angry. Instead, a glint of admiration shone in his eyes.

"I'll call a meeting with the nobles; we need tae send as many men north as we can to launch an attack on Tarag and his men. I'm estimating it'll take us a day—perhaps two—tae get enough men for that. While most of us march north, we need tae keep enough men here tae protect the castle and surrounding lands in case his men retaliate."

Eadan gave him a slow nod, looking pleased.

"'Tis a sound plan. Ye handled this well, Ronan. Moireach told me what a fine job ye've done with the castle matters as well."

Ronan looked at him, astonishment rendering him still. Eadan chuckled.

"Moireach has a stern manner, but he likes ye. He says he's seen the change in ye over these past few weeks, and ye've taken the responsibility well."

Relief and pride filtered in through the ever-present cloud of self-doubt and uncertainty that had plagued him ever since Eadan left him in charge. He tentatively returned his cousin's smile.

Eadan turned his focus to Kara, approaching her as she stood. He bowed in greeting, his curious gaze pinned on her face.

"Ye have the same accent as my wife," he said cautiously.

"I've heard," Kara said, sliding a glance to Ronan.

"May I ask where ye're from?" Eadan asked.

Kara looked at Ronan, and he gave her a small nod.

"I suspect I'm from the same place as your bride," Kara said. "Or rather, I should say . . . the same time."

CHAPTER 22

*K*ara stood stock-still, studying her fellow time traveler from head to toe.

On the surface, Fiona Macleay looked like a fourteenth-century noblewoman in the fine green gown she wore, but the way she spoke was pure twenty-first century American. Fiona took her in with an equal measure of astonishment, and Kara suspected she was thinking the same thing about her.

She had come to the castle with Eadan and Ronan after they'd revealed to him she was a time traveler. Eadan had looked only mildly astonished, given that he'd already encountered—and married —a time traveler. Kara guessed it would take much more to surprise him at this point. Ronan and Eadan were meeting with the nobles in the great hall, and Ronan had brought her to Fiona's private chamber to introduce her, leaving them alone with a cryptic, *ye both have much tae discuss.*

"So. Should I go first?" Fiona asked with a wry grin, and Kara took an instant liking to her.

They sat on two chairs by the window as Fiona told her how she'd come to this time—discovering Tairseach, spotting a woman among the ruins, the tug of wind, her falling in love with Eadan, and her decision to stay.

Kara told her everything that happened since discovering Alice's letter in her attic. When Kara finished, Fiona slowly shook her head.

"I know you're probably wondering if I've any clue of how this all works, but I don't. If a druid witch performed some sort of spell, if it was Tairseach itself . . . I don't know. I wish I had answers. I've been here for months now, but sometimes I feel the need to pinch myself when I wake up," Fiona said.

"But . . . you chose to stay," Kara said. "Do you miss the twenty-first century? Indoor plumbing?" she added with a small smile.

"You get used to things here a lot quicker than you realize," Fiona said. "And for Eadan, I was happy to give up all those things. As strange as this was at first . . . I feel like I've always belonged here. He's the love of my life. Once I realized that, it made the decision easy."

Kara studied her with envy. She loved Ronan but held no illusions he felt the same. He cared about her more than any of his other mistresses, and he desired her, but that was the extent of his feelings for her.

And even if he did love her, could she give up her life in the present day?

What life? she wondered. *The life where you're a jobless lonely journalist with no close family and few friends, where the man you love lives centuries in the past and is long dead?*

"It's not an easy decision," Fiona said gently, noticing the turbulence in Kara's eyes. "But if I could go back . . . I would have tried to get here sooner. My life was so empty and I didn't realize it. I was searching for something in my own time, and I didn't realize for what. Not until I met him. Traveling through time—it course corrected my path . . . and now I'm where I'm supposed to be."

Fiona's words echoed Kara's past feelings. Hadn't she felt the same in her own life? A gnawing emptiness she tried to fill with her job?

"Well, I'm not going anywhere until I find my family," Kara said finally, getting to her feet. "I haven't made any progress. I wonder about causality—did the fact that they died in my own time mean I've already failed?"

"I tried thinking about causality, but it made my brain hurt," Fiona said with a chuckle. "Especially considering there may be magic involved in all this. I've just come to the conclusion that things are the way they were meant to be."

"Which means . . . my family will die and

there's nothing I can do," Kara said, alarm coursing through her.

"No, that's not what I'm saying. But I do think your presence in this time means something," Fiona said. "From what you've told me, just you being here has helped Ronan figure out who's behind the threats to the clan. Maybe you've already put events into motion that will stop the conflict that kills them."

Kara moved to the window, looking out at the bustling castle grounds. She hoped Fiona was right, but she couldn't rely on guesswork. There had to be something more she could do.

"What if I'm missing something?" Kara mused aloud. "What if I've been looking in the wrong place? None of the land deeds or the rents mention a Suibhne or Orla. And Ronan's sent messengers to nearby villages."

Kara froze as a thought suddenly struck her. She whirled to face Fiona.

"What if they're not in any of the villages? I know there isn't much fertile ground around here, but are there isolated farms nearby?"

"From what I've seen, most people live in villages," Fiona hedged. "Isolated farms are few and far between. But there are some."

Kara's heart picked up its pace; hope swelled in her chest.

"Maybe I haven't found my family because I've been looking in the wrong places."

SHE DIDN'T GET a chance to talk to Ronan about her revelation right away. He, Eadan, and many of the nobles left the castle after their meeting. Luag told her they were gathering men from surrounding villages to head up north, and he wanted her to remain at the castle rather than return to the manor, there was more protection here.

So she spent most the day with Fiona, whom she grew to like even more. She realized that if she'd met Fiona in her own time, they would have become fast friends. They shared details of their lives in the future; Fiona told her about her friend Isabelle, that she hoped she'd received her letter and knew she was safe. Kara told her she hadn't seen a letter when she'd arrived at the castle in Tairseach; hopefully someone had discovered the letter and sent it to Isabelle. Fiona's eyes glistened at this, a relieved smile tugging at her lips.

When Ronan returned to the castle, it wasn't until after supper, and she found him in his guest chamber. She approached, eager to tell him her new plan for finding her family, but froze at the dark look in Ronan's eyes.

"What's wrong?"

"We couldnae gather many men for the march north on such short notice. I'm a feared we willnae have the numbers tae remove Tarag's men from our lands. Kara . . . ye need tae return tae yer own time."

A stab of hurt pierced her. She squared her shoulders, her mouth tight.

"I'm not leaving until I find my family. I was going to tell you—I think I've been looking in the wrong places for them. I want to check the farms in this area."

"Ye can take Luag with ye, and then have him escort ye to Tairseach."

"Ronan—"

"'Tis for yer safety, Kara. Tarag kens what ye look like; ye'll be a target if I fall in battle."

Pain spiraled through her at the thought of Ronan's death. She took a breath and stepped forward, holding his gaze.

"Fiona stayed with Eadan. She's staying now—I assume he's not sending her away."

Ask me to stay, Kara pleaded silently. *Give me a reason to stay.*

Something shifted in Ronan's eyes, and he looked away.

"'Tis different with Eadan and Fiona," he muttered. "They love each other and are bound through marriage."

Kara blinked back a wave of tears, trying not to show how much his words gutted her. He couldn't have made his lack of feelings for her more clear. She'd been foolish to hope he felt anything more.

"I've told Eadan and my men tae escort ye back tae Tairseach, with or without yer agreement, tae get ye back tae yer own time should I fall in battle," he continued, still not looking at her. "And my men ken tae look for yer family. I'm keeping men in this area while we march tae prevent Tarag's men from doing harm tae the locals. Once we're gone, my men will make sure yer family is safe, and they'll not give up the search until they're found."

"And—and what if the battle is a success?" she asked. She didn't know why she was twisting the knife in her own heart, but she recklessly continued, "Will you still want me to return to my own time?"

"'Tis not yer time, Kara," he said, his tone wavering. "And ye told me yerself . . . ye're here for one thing."

He searched her eyes, as if daring her to challenge his words. *That was before I knew I loved you,* she wanted to shout, but pride kept her silent.

"We'll spend the night in the castle—there's more protection for ye here. Tomorrow, while I march north, Luag will escort ye tae the farms. And then . . . and then ye're tae return tae yer time."

He hesitated before turning, but she reached out to grip his hand. If he was determined to send her away, she wouldn't stop him. After she searched the farms and her family wasn't there, what more could she do? She trusted that Ronan wouldn't give up the search; Eadan and Fiona would help as well.

But she could have one last night with him. One last night to savor every part of him, to burn onto her memory, something she could hold on to across the chasm of time.

"Stay with me tonight," she whispered.

He stilled, and for several taut moments she feared her would refuse her. But Ronan reached out to pull her against his chest, his eyes a storm of emotion as he lowered his mouth to seize hers. His kiss was fierce, his tongue probing her mouth as he stripped her of her clothes, only releasing her to remove his tunic and kilt.

He carried her to the bed, and even as sparks of pleasure raced through her, she kept her eyes open and on him, wanting to relish every moment of their last moments together. He kept his eyes trained on hers as well as he suckled on her breasts, before peppering kisses down her abdomen to taste her, moaning as she twisted and writhed on the bed, as if his tongue was a conductor and her body the orchestra, reacting to its every move. His mouth remained on her center even as she climaxed, keeping his golden eyes trained on her face, as if he too was memorizing and taking in every detail of her pleasure.

Only then did he lift her so that she straddled him, sinking her down onto his erection. She began to undulate on him as he reached up to grab her breasts, his breath coming fast and hard between clenched teeth.

"My witch; my Kara," he gasped, as she rode him, reaching down to grip his broad shoulders, the movement of their bodies building to a crescendo of pleasure.

She cried out as her orgasm tore through her,

and he reached up to grip her waist as his own climax roiled through him. Their bodies remained locked as they shook and trembled their mutual release.

She sank down onto the bed next to him, breathless, remnant love and desire coursing through her.

Ronan pulled her close, burying his face in her hair, whispering words that broke her heart.

"I'm only sending ye away for yer safety. Live yer life, my Kara. I'll never forget ye."

"And I'll never forget you," she whispered, her voice breaking as she looked up to meet his eyes.

I love you, Ronan of Clan Macleay. Always.

CHAPTER 23

*A*s Ronan rode away from the castle, he tried not to think of his golden goddess. Her soft skin against his as he made love to her, the pain in her eyes when he urged her to go back to her time.

It was first light the next morning, and he'd slipped out of their bed as she slept, unable to bear saying a final goodbye to her. He'd done that with his body and mouth the night before, trying to show her how much he loved her, how much she'd affected him.

'Tis for the best, he told himself. She needed to return to her own time, free of clan conflicts and the threat of Tarag.

He'd come close to telling her he loved her the night before. But he'd kept the words to himself. If he told her how he felt, she may have considered staying in a dangerous time she didn't belong.

"Yer thinking of Kara," Eadan observed, pulling him from the tumult of his thoughts.

Ronan glanced over at his cousin who rode along his side. A small contingent of men rode behind them as they made their way north.

"I'm always thinking of her. I'll always think of her," Ronan said, keeping his voice low so that the men around them couldn't hear. "But it doesnae matter. She's returning tae her own time. I donnae ken how ye convinced Fiona tae stay, but I'll not do that tae her."

"I told Fiona tae go back as well. She refused. Ye should've told the lass how ye feel."

"She doesnae belong in this time. 'Tis not safe," Ronan replied, shuttering his pain away. "She's going tae Tairseach today and returning tae her time."

Eadan fell silent. Ronan was grateful his cousin didn't press the matter. But still, thoughts of Kara remained during their journey north, and it wasn't until they reached the outskirts of their northern lands that he forced her image from his mind, stiffening at the sight of Tarag and his men.

He counted roughly one hundred men gathered with Tarag; only slightly more than their contingent of seventy men. They weren't as outnumbered as he'd feared, but unease still darted through him at the sight of Tarag's men, who'd dismounted from their horses and stood posed for battle. Ronan had fought before, in small skirmishes during other clan conflicts, and he'd fought

Dughall's men alongside Eadan, but this battle seemed more ominous.

Because it's the first battle ye've spearheaded, he realized. When he'd fought in the past, it had been at the behest of Eadan or some other clan noble. This was the first time his leadership had called for fighting. He could only pray that the men who'd followed him and Eadan into battle would emerge victorious.

As they drew closer, Ronan froze. A dead man lay sprawled across the flank of Tarag's horse.

Keeping his gaze on Ronan, Tarag mounted the horse and rode across the broad field to meet them. The dead man was James, the same man Kara had flirted with for information.

Dread filling his gut, he and Eadan rode ahead to meet Tarag in the center of the field. When they reached Tarag, he shoved James' body to the ground.

"Ye didnae think I would figure out who revealed our secrets?" Tarag demanded with a sneer, his focus on Ronan. "But I have tae admit . . . 'twas clever getting yer whore to ply my man for information. Donnae fret, after my men take out yers, the punishment I have in mind for yer Kara is a pleasurable one."

Rage surged through Ronan, and he had to restrain himself from charging forward and spearing Tarag through with his sword. Eadan seemed to sense Ronan's anger and gave him a look of caution before he spoke.

"My cousin has told me what's happened in my absence. Despite yer treachery, I offer ye one last chance tae resolve this off the battlefield," Eadan said.

Tarag laughed, withdrawing his sword.

"I offer *ye* this last chance to get off the lands we've claimed. We've paid off the farmers who toil these lands. They're happy tae have us here, not absentee landlords like ye and yer clan from the south. Ye're the ones who choose bloodshed. Or," he added with a wicked smile, his eyes glittering as he once again focused on Ronan, "my offer from yer first visit stands. My Elspeth recently had an . . . accident, leaving me a widower and my bed cold."

Ronan froze, horror snaking through him. He doubted Elspeth had met an accident. Tarag had gotten the information he needed from her about Clan Macleay and killed her. The bastard was evil, down to his bones.

"Give me that delicious golden-haired whore of yers tae enjoy," Tarag continued, his eyes burning into Ronan's, "and perhaps all will be forgiven."

This time, Ronan couldn't quell his rage. He unsheathed his sword. His action was a signal to the other men the battle had begun, and Eadan shouted for their men to charge.

Ronan's focus was only on Tarag. He leapt from his horse and darted toward Tarag. Their swords clashed in midair as they began to fight.

Around him, men from both sides clashed in battle, swords clanging, blades spearing through flesh, grunts and cries of fury and pain surrounding them.

Tarag met each of Ronan's sword clashes with his own. He suddenly reached out to kick Ronan, sending him sprawling to the ground.

Ronan landed with such force the pain seared his insides. He scrambled for his sword as Tarag stepped forward, raising his sword, his face contorted with murderous fury.

Ronan's sword was just out of reach; he didn't have time to ward off the blow. The only emotion that filled his chest was a painful, burning regret; regret that he would never see his Kara again, regret that he'd never told her how he much he loved her. *I love ye, my Kara,* he thought, as Tarag's sword careened toward his heart.

But all at once the sword was gone. Ronan looked up, startled. Eadan had knocked Tarag to the ground. He helped Ronan to his feet, handing him his sword as they charged at Tarag together.

But one of Tarag's men intercepted Eadan's path, and Ronan was once again alone with Tarag, a surge of renewed strength flowing through him. He wanted to survive—not just for his clan and their lands. But for Kara.

His momentary brush with death had forced him to realize that he needed to get back to Kara, to tell her that he loved her and wanted her by his side. For all of his days.

Tarag growled, charging forward. Ronan dodged his blow, using the opportunity to kick out at Tarag's knees. Tarag fell hard, but angled his sword toward Ronan's chest. Ronan caught the sword with his bare hand, ignoring the scorching pain as his skin tore and bled.

Holding Tarag's sword with his bare hand, he raised his sword and sank it into Tarag's chest. Tarag let out a pained roar, falling back onto the ground as Ronan removed the sword. Ronan stared down at the dying man, not looking away until the light left his eyes.

He took no pleasure in taking another man's life, even a man such as Tarag, but a sense of relief filled him as Tarag drew his last breath. His death meant he couldn't hurt anyone—including his Kara —again.

Ronan turned to join Eadan as he fought one of Tarag's men, but many of Tarag's men had seen their leader fall, and it turned the tide of the battle. Some continued to fight while others fled.

It did not take long to defeat the rest of Tarag's men; the men of Clan Macleay were emboldened by Tarag's death, and soon the battle was over.

A powerful surge of relief filled his chest; there would be matters to tend to in the aftermath, but the battle with Tarag was over. Only one person dominated his thoughts now. Kara.

She may have already gone to Tairseach, back to her own time and from him, because he'd been too much of a fool to tell her he loved her.

One thing was certain now, a certainty that filled him ever since Tarag's sword had careened toward his heart—his life was not worth living without his Kara. And he needed to tell her. If there was still time.

He turned, on the verge of telling his cousin he was going to Tairseach, when a horse suddenly charged onto the field. He whirled to face it, his sword at the ready.

But Ronan stilled. He recognized the rider—it was a messenger from the castle. Panic gripped him and he raced forward.

"Tarag's men," the messenger said, out of breath. "They waited 'til ye and Eadan were away. They've set fire tae our lands."

CHAPTER 24

*A*nxiety coiled around Kara, holding her tightly in its grip as she made her way through the countryside on horseback along with Fiona and Luag. They'd spent the morning venturing to isolated farms in the countryside, inquiring about a Suibhne and Orla.

They'd come across three farms, and no one had heard of them. After the third farm, Kara began to fear she wouldn't find her family after all, that the hands of fate were working against her, and what had happened in the past was impossible to prevent.

But that wasn't the sole reason for her anxiety. She was worried about Ronan, fighting against Tarag and his men in the north. What if he fell in battle? Grief speared her chest at the thought, and she tightened her grip on the reins of her horse. Alice's letter had mentioned no battle nor its outcome.

There's still hope, Kara tried to reassure herself. *For your family, and for Ronan.*

She glanced over at Fiona, who was silent and pale. She'd tried to maintain an upbeat façade, but Kara knew she was worried about Eadan.

They approached yet another farm, and Kara braced herself for disappointment. There were only two other farms in the area after this one and then it would be time to give up her search.

I tried, Alice, Kara said silently, grief and regret surging through her. *I tried to find them.*

But she froze as a young woman exited the small cottage up ahead, clutching a bucket. She bore an eerie resemblance to a younger Alice— blond hair, fine features, green eyes. Kara's heart picked up its pace and she allowed a sliver of hope to crawl through her. *Could it be?*

Kara dismounted, handing her reins to Luag and hurrying toward the woman.

"Orla?" Kara asked, her voice wavering.

The woman stopped, lowering the bucket to the ground and eyeing her with curiosity.

"Aye," she replied, as Kara's heart leapt into her throat. "Is there something I can help ye with?"

Kara sat opposite Orla and her husband Suib-hne, a dark-haired man in his late twenties with kind eyes, trying not to show the level of her excitement. In the corner of the small cottage, Fiona sat opposite their two young daughters, speaking to them in quiet tones. Luag stood outside the cottage.

"Ye're saying we're in danger?" Suibhne asked, his brows knitted together in a frown.

Kara had told them the same story they'd used with the other farmers: the laird of Macleay Castle had sent his wife, her companion, and their trusted guard instead of a messenger as his men had been called north to fight. They'd warned them of a possible attack on their lands from a rival clan while the battle raged in the north, and the farmers should evacuate for their safety. With the other farmers, Luag had done most of the talking so as to not draw suspicion or distrust at Fiona and Kara's strange accents.

But this time, Kara did the talking. It was important to her that she deliver this news herself, accent be damned.

"Yes," Kara said, trying to keep her voice steady, when she wanted to scream, *I came from the future to save your lives.*

"We just moved here days ago," Orla said with a sigh. "We cannae afford tae move again."

Kara stiffened with surprise. Not only had she not been looking in the right place for them, they hadn't moved here yet. They must have just moved here before the fire that killed them—in the original timeline. *Not in this one,* Kara thought with a rush of determination.

"You don't have to leave permanently. Just for a

few days until the threat is over," Kara said. "Is there somewhere you can go?"

"My cousin lives in Inverness," Suibhne said, after a brief pause.

Inverness. That was where the other branch of her family lived, the branch that she descended from.

"Go there," Kara urged. "I'll make sure the laird sends for you once it's safe. You have my word."

She stiffened, nervous that they'd argue with her and refuse, but they gave her reluctant nods.

"If you don't mind, we'll wait while you pack. I can help," Kara offered. She wouldn't feel at ease until she saw them evacuate with her own two eyes.

"'Tis kind of ye tae offer, but we can pack our things. We donnae have much in the way of belongings," Orla said, giving her a polite smile. As Suibhne rose, Orla lingered at the table. "Ye seem familiar. Do I ken ye somehow?"

I'm your distant cousin from the twenty-first century.

"No," Kara replied, smiling. "I'm from the south of England. I have a familiar face, I suppose."

Orla gave her one last look before turning to help Suibhne gather their things.

Kara and Fiona left the cottage, standing outside with Luag while Suibhne and Orla packed. She listened to the soft tone of Orla's voice as she spoke to her daughters, the bell-like laughter of the two young girls.

Tears pricked at her eyes; tears of relief and

gratitude. In another timeline, they would have died violently in a fire. Fiona seemed to sense Kara's undercurrent of emotions and reached out to grip her hand. Kara squeezed it, relieved that there was another time traveler in this time, someone who understood the implication of what was happening.

"The laird will make certain your farm is looked after while you're gone," Kara assured Suibhne and Orla, moments later, after they'd loaded their few belongings onto their wagon. They sat perched on the wagon with their horse, ready to go. "He'll send for you once it's safe."

Suibhne gave her a nod of gratitude, while Orla kept her eyes trained on Kara's as they rode away. Kara could tell that Orla somehow sensed they were linked. *You have no idea,* she thought.

"I did it, Alice," Kara whispered, as if her grand-mother could hear her across the chasm of time. "We did it."

But the tension in her body lingered. Her family was safe, but Ronan's fate remained uncertain.

They mounted their horses and made their way back to the castle. But as they made their way down the dirt road, Kara stiffened. She could smell acrid flames in the air, and alarm skittered through her.

Fire.

*a*t Kara's side, Fiona and Luag tensed—
they'd smelled the flames as well.

"Stay behind me!" Luag shouted, kicking the
sides of his horse as he rode out ahead of them.
Kara and Fiona exchanged nervous looks before
trailing him down the dirt road.

Kara's heart thundered furiously as they rode.
Was this the fire Alice had written about in her
letter? She had saved her family—but what about
the other lives in this area?

They kept riding in silence, their horses' hooves
pounding the ground and their frantic breaths the
only sounds. The scent of smoke grew stronger,
becoming overwhelming as they reached the
outskirts of the village.

Fiona gasped, her hand flying to her mouth.
Kara froze, taking in the sight before them.

Several buildings in the center of the village
had been set aflame—a couple of merchants' shops

and the tavern. A dozen men were dousing the fire with buckets of water while other men evacuated villagers from the surrounding cottages.

Luag dismounted and tied his horse to a post, shouting for them to stay here out of harm's way while he helped the men douse the fire.

"Doesn't he know me by now?" Kara grumbled, dismounting from her horse. She wouldn't sit still while a fire raged; she could at least help evacuate the villagers.

Fiona dismounted as well, and they both hurried to the edge of the village square. The frightened villagers streamed out; many seemed to recognize Fiona, giving her grateful smiles.

"If you've nowhere to go, come to the castle," Fiona told the villagers, raising her voice so they could hear her over the chaos of the fire. "We'll let you know when it's safe to return."

Fiona turned to Kara, lowering her voice. "Is this what your grandmother said would happen?"

"Yes," Kara said slowly, her eyes going to the fire, which seemed to be dying thanks to the joint efforts of the men dousing it with water. They must have gotten to it quickly before it could spread. "But . . .it happened differently in her letter. She mentioned the fire taking place in the middle of the night—that's what local records indicated."

A chill went through her as she imagined the damage that would have done—such a fire taking place in the middle of the night. Especially if it spread to the countryside, killing those living in isolated farms. *Like my family,* Kara realized in a daze.

"Then it looks like you've already changed history," Fiona whispered, giving a polite nod to an elderly woman and her husband as they walked past.

Kara stilled, allowing Fiona's words to settle. Ronan's men were monitoring the surrounding countryside to prevent any more fires or damage Tarag's men could try to start. Her eyes went back to the fire, now dying even more quickly with the joint efforts of the men.

Her actions in this time may not have prevented Tarag's men from acting, but she changed the timing of their action, which saved lives. She didn't know which of her actions had caused this—getting the information from Ronan's man, insisting that Ronan investigate Dughall's allies—but they had changed the events in this time.

She'd done what she came here to do. She'd honored Alice's wish and could make her way back to Tairseach as Ronan had directed, and return to her own time.

To a time where Ronan didn't exist.

Grief seized her heart at the thought, and she closed her eyes.

"You did it, Kara," Fiona said with a concerned frown, misinterpreting her tears. "You stopped the—"

"It's not that," Kara whispered. "It's . . . Ronan. I

love him."

Fiona's expression softened. "I know."

"You know?"

"I was once in the same position as you," Fiona said, smiling, "and I think you already know what decision you're going to make. Your heart has already decided for you."

Kara swallowed, tears blurring her vision.

Fiona was right. The moment she realized she loved Ronan was the moment she knew in her heart she would stay in this time. And she felt, deep down, that she'd already done all she could in her own time. With Alice gone, there was nothing for her there. Perhaps, if Ronan and Eadan agreed, Clan Macleay could use someone with her investigative skills.

She would stay where her heart was, where a part of her already felt she belonged. Here in this time. With Ronan.

"And look," Fiona said, her eyes lighting up as she looked at something past Kara's shoulder. "Right on cue."

Kara turned, and her heart leapt into her throat. Ronan approached the village on horseback with Eadan and several of his men. Other than his hand, wrapped with a piece of torn plaid, he had no noticeable injuries.

The wave of relief that swept over her was so great she nearly sank to her knees.

Ronan spotted her at the same time she did, and his entire face lit up. She stumbled toward him without realizing it as Ronan dismounted and strode toward her in several large strides, pulling her into his arms, pressing his lips to hers.

Kara clung to him as the world around them faded away, and she returned his kiss. Ronan was here, in her arms, alive.

When they finally broke apart, Ronan rested his forehead on hers.

"Tarag is dead. The battle is won," he whispered, and another surge of relief filled her. "Kara, I ken I told ye tae return tae yer own time, but please. Donnae. And not just because Tarag is dead. Because I love ye."

Kara's heart soared. She pulled back, blinking up at him. She needed to hear the words again.

"What?"

"I love ye, Kara. My witch from a time that has yet tae come," Ronan whispered. "I—I ken 'tis selfish of me tae ask ye tae stay," he continued, taking her hands and pressing them against his chest. "But I love ye with everything I am. I want tae spend the rest of my days with ye at my side. Stay. Yer a part of me, and without ye I'm mere shadow." His voice wavered, his golden eyes shining with tears.

"Ronan . . ." she whispered.

He stiffened, as if bracing himself for her refusal. But she smiled. Wide.

"I love you too. And I'm not going anywhere."

Stark relief filled his eyes, and he swung her up in his arms, pressing his lips to hers.

He set her back down to the ground. Out of the corner of her eye, she could see Eadan and Fiona standing arm in arm, watching them with smiles. The fire had died down completely, and many of the villagers were giving them curious looks.

But right now, her entire world was Ronan. Ronan pulled her close into the circle of his arms, his golden eyes pinning hers.

"Will ye marry me, Kara? Will ye be my bride?"

"Yes," she said, beaming. "With all my heart, yes. But first . . . there's something I need to do."

Hours later, Ronan's arms were secure around her waist as they rode toward Tairseach. Fiona told her it looked the same in this time as it did in present day, but it was still startling to see the very same village she'd driven her car to weeks ago.

Once they reached the ruins, they dismounted, Ronan tying his horse to a tree. Kara looked down at the two letters in her hands. One letter was to Jon. She'd written a letter similar to the letter Fiona had written to her friend Isabelle, that she was safe and happy in Scotland, and to not look for her. The other letter was addressed . . . to Alice.

Of the many unanswered questions she had, the one which plagued her the most was *how* Alice knew she could time travel. And the answer was so starkly simple that Kara couldn't believe she hadn't figured it out before.

Kara had been the one to tell her.

At some point in the future, Alice would receive the letter Kara just wrote, and it would set into motion the events that led Kara to coming to this time—to saving her family, and to meeting Ronan. And somehow, Kara wasn't sure how, she would arrange to have Kara's letter to Jon sent after her death—and after Kara traveled back in time. She was certain of this, and she could only conclude that as a time traveler there was some base instinct in her that made her aware of such things.

What she wasn't sure of was exactly how the druid witch would affect her future time travel. Maybe the witch had just given her the final push into this time. She recalled the name of her voice on the wind, right before she'd traveled through time. *Kara.*

And she recalled Alice's lack of concern about her love life and absence of meaningful relationships, how often Alice had told her everything would work out in the end. It was because Alice knew Kara would one day go back in time and meet her soul mate.

And that she would stay.

"Are ye ready?"

She looked up at Ronan and smiled. She'd told him what she realized, and though he'd looked disconcerted at first, he now understood.

Ronan took her hand and together they made their way to the ruins of the castle. As she drew near, the wind picked up, and she wondered if it was the same wind that pulled her out of her own time and into this one.

Ronan didn't seem to notice or hear the wind, but his grip on her hand tightened, as if frightened that she would disappear, pulled through the veil of time. She returned his tight grip, as if he were a temporal anchor holding her still. She knelt, placing the two letters on the ground.

She didn't know how this worked; Fiona told her she left her letter to Isabelle at the castle and it soon disappeared, hopefully pulled through time.

She stepped back, keeping her eyes on the letters, Ronan's hand still clutching hers. The wind increased, whipping around her hair. Astonishment and relief roiled through her as the letters vanished, where they would arrive in the future, where Alice would find them . . . and lead an unknowing Kara to where she belonged.

At her side, Ronan's eyes went wide and his lips parted at the sight of the letters vanishing. The wind stilled, and Kara's shoulders relaxed. She squeezed his hand, and he seemed to come down from his surprise, meeting her gaze with a smile.

"Take me home, Ronan."

CHAPTER 26

Present Day
Chicago, Illinois

*P*lease don't try to find me, Izzy. I'm happy. Happier than I've ever been. I wish I could tell you more. But know that I will always think of you.

   Love,
   Fiona

Isabelle read over the letter for the millionth time, raking her hand through her hair with a sigh. She'd received Fiona's letter out of the blue two weeks ago.

Fiona had gone missing in Scotland over two months ago, and her letter didn't ease Isabelle's worry. For one thing, the letter was written on pieces of ancient-looking parchment and had arrived with no return address. And for another, it wasn't like Fiona to just disappear and not tell her where she was going, only to send her a letter weeks later insisting she was fine and to not look for her.

Guilt prickled at Isabelle's spine. It was her idea for Fiona to go on her honeymoon to Scotland solo after she'd called off her wedding to her fiancé Derek. If she hadn't suggested it, maybe Fiona would be here now.

Isabelle had flown to Scotland to meet up with Fiona. But when Fiona didn't meet up with her in Edinburgh as planned, Isabelle immediately searched for her, filing reports with the police in both Scotland, and then Chicago when she'd reluctantly returned home after making no progress finding Fiona in Scotland. She called both police departments on a daily basis, but no progress had been made. She knew if she gave the police Fiona's letter, they would officially close her case.

When Fiona first went missing, she thought that maybe she'd run off with her ex-fiancé and was too ashamed to tell Isabelle. But when Isabelle went to see him, he had no idea where she was, and looked genuinely worried when she told him Fiona was missing.

Fiona had no close family left, so it was just Isabelle doing all the searching. And now this letter had shown up with no return address. Though Isabelle recognized the carefully looped handwriting as Fiona's, something about the letter just seemed . . . off.

She again looked down at the letter as a

memory struck her. In one of the towns in the Highlands where she'd stopped during her search for Fiona, an innkeeper had told her about the rumors of a nearby medieval town that lay in ruins, a town that not everyone had the ability to see. It was called Tairseach, which meant "portal" in Gaelic. The innkeeper told her the rumors of disappearances around the area went back centuries.

Isabelle had thanked the innkeeper, though her heart had sunk. She'd assumed the rumors were just superstitious nonsense.

But now a chill crept down her spine. Was it nonsense? Or could there be something to the rumors?

She picked up the letter, clutching it to her chest. Fiona was her best friend, and she wouldn't stop looking for her if the tables were turned. Even if she got a mysterious letter claiming otherwise. There was only one thing to do.

It was time to return to Scotland.

Buy Ciaran's Bond (Highlander Fate Book 3) now. Keep reading for a brief excerpt.

"I'm called Ciaran," he said. "Ciaran of—"

He abruptly stopped himself, and a shadow passed over his face.

"I'm Isabelle," she said, filling the awkward silence.

"Isabelle," he said slowly, and something about the way he said her name made a sharp spike of awareness pierce her. "Allow me tae escort ye back tae my camp."

Isabelle followed him, shaking her head as if to rid herself of the spark of desire she'd felt when he said her name. She'd possibly landed in another time; there was no time to swoon over a mysterious Scot in medieval clothing.

She took several deep breaths to calm herself as they walked. Her brain still protested the notion of having traveled back through time, but there was nothing she could do until she could at least see her surroundings. And then, God willing, she'd find a road—and a way back to Tairseach. Kensa had some answering to do.

They reached a clearing, and Ciaran placed a plaid cloak on the ground by a small fire. He straightened, pointing across the clearing.

"I'll be over there. If ye need food or drink, there's some in that bag over there. If ye want tae get out of yer muddy clothes, I have a fresh tunic in that bag as well. 'Tis long enough that ye can wear it as a gown."

Isabelle nodded her thanks as he made his way across the clearing and out of sight. Once he was gone, she reached into his bag, freezing as she pulled out a tunic. This certainly didn't look like a piece of modern clothing. It looked homemade, but by someone who knew how to stitch well, and made of a comfortable wool fabric.

She shed her dirty clothes and slid on the tunic, settling down onto her makeshift bed. She stared up at the starry night sky, hoping against hope for the sight of a plane or anything that signaled she was still in the twenty-first century. But there were only the multitude of stars and the darkness of the night sky.

There's a reasonable explanation, Isabelle told herself firmly, closing her eyes. *There has to be.*

Isabelle awoke the next morning with a start. She sat up, her body aching from sleeping on the ground. She looked around with a sinking feeling. She'd hoped that it had all been a dream. But she was still in the same clearing, wearing a medieval tunic.

She got to her feet, crossing the clearing to where Ciaran had disappeared to the night before. He could help her get to the nearest road back to Tairseach. But she didn't find him, and for a moment panic filled her as she wondered if he'd left.

She heard splashing in the stream, and her heart soared with relief.

Isabelle followed the sound downstream and froze when she found Ciaran.

Ciaran was cleaning himself off in the stream . . . completely naked. The filth and grime that covered him the night before had hidden a sculpted, muscular body—from a pair of long tapered legs, firm abdominal muscles, broad shoulders, and a rippling back. He was faced away from her, thank God, and didn't seem to notice she was there as he washed himself with his hands.

Isabelle swallowed, wondering how she should make herself known, but she was unable to speak. Ciaran turned, and the simmering desire that burned within her skyrocketed. The grime and darkness of the night before had concealed not only a stunning body, but a strikingly handsome face. He had a generous mouth, a chiseled jaw dusted with a couple of days' growth of stubble, and an aristocratic nose. He opened his eyes, and Isabelle had to stifle a gasp. His eyes were even more dazzling in daylight—their grays and greens highlighted in the sun. He was by far the most beautiful man she had ever seen.

It was only the look of shock in Ciaran's stunning eyes that brought her back to herself. She turned away from him, swallowing hard.

"I—I'm sorry," she stammered. "I didn't see you when I awoke, so I came to find you."

"'Tis all right, lass," he said, and she could have sworn she heard a trace of amusement in his voice.

A long stretch of silence passed, and she hoped —prayed—that he was getting dressed. Soon, she felt his hand on her shoulder, turning her to face him.

He was even more handsome up close. Those multicolored eyes of his were trained on hers with intense focus. She took a step back, painfully aware of how she must look. Her dark hair was mussed, there were still traces of grime on her skin from the muddy stream, and she must have smelled awful.

"Sorry," she said again, stupidly. She noticed with annoyance that he was only half dressed; he wore a belted plaid kilt, and his glistening muscled abdomen was way too close to her body. She took another step back. "Ah—are you going to put a shirt on?"

He moved past her and shrugged into a tunic he'd strewn over a log. Isabelle expelled a small sigh of relief. At least now she could concentrate.

"Now that it's light," Isabelle said, "can you

direct me—or help me find—a road? If I could just—"

"Quiet," Ciaran interrupted, moving to stand in front of her.

Isabelle stilled, startled at his sudden state of alarm.

And then she heard it too. Footsteps approaching them through the trees.

Two men stepped out, their hands on the hilts of their swords, their eyes gleaming with dark intent.

ALSO BY STELLA KNIGHT

ABOUT THE AUTHOR

Stella Knight writes time travel romance and historical romance novels. She enjoys transporting readers to different times and places with vivid, nuanced heroes and heroines.

She resides in sunny southern California with her own swoon-worthy hero and her collection of too many books and board games. She's been writing for as long as she can remember, and when not writing, she can be found traveling to new locales, diving into a new book, or watching her favorite film or documentary. She loves romance, history, mystery, and adventure, all of which you'll find in her books.

Stay in touch!
stellaknightbooks.com